Friendship Productions
M105
present
on Ledges "WEEKEND IN
★ ★ ★ featuring ★
ODD RUND
and UTOPIA
E PRAIRIE LEAGUE
PEOPLE * BUZZY LINHART
JULY 4th - 12noon
tes open 9:30A.M. July 4th)
RAIN or SHINE
Tickets available at the gate, day of show only $6.50
FREE PARKING
NO OVERNIGHT CAMPING !!!
MW01681201
Live Rock Nite Club!
FAYREWETHER
General admission $2.50
Polydor Recording Artists
LEFT END plus BABY-O
Presenting a special Christmas extravagan
Cleveland's #1 Rock and Roll Band
EASY STREET
Dozens of guest appearances
PRESENT
ROBIN TROWER
LITTLE RICHARD
STAMPEDERS
VIKING SALOON'S
DEPENDENCE WEEKEND
RTY THIS FRI., SAT. & SUN.
INDEPENDENCE DAY DRINK PRICES
EVERY NIGHT 8:30 to MIDNIGHT
FRI.
I DON'T CARE
SAT.
LOVER'S LANE
SUN.
BLUESTON
Jonah Koslen and
BREATHLESS
CHARLIE WEINER
MARIONETTE
MILES BOOZER
FREE
DMISSION
PLENTY OF FREE PARKING
OWEST BEV. & FOOD PRICES IN TOWN!
FOR A QUICKY (OR TWO) BEFORE
NG YOUR FAVORITE SPOT DOWN
HE "FLATS" (CHECK US OUT)
AFTER HOURS BREAKFAST DANCE ALL NIGHT WITH LIVE ENTERTAINMENT.
THE "GLADIATORS" MALE DANCE GROUP NITELY
BURT REYNOLDS LOOK—ALIKE CONTEST.
CKY'S-top of the flats
NEW CORRAL
THURSDAY
Ladies Nite! Ladies admitted Free!
ORION
FRIDAY
DESTINY
SATURDAY
FAYREWETHER
SUNDAY
LOVE AFFAIR
Radio Recording Artists
FRI · SAT · HAPPY HOUR
jazz
FORECAST
MOONLIGHT DRIVE

Media and Reviewer Comments about Greg Cielec,
My Cleveland Story, Home and Away Games
and *A Poem on a Bar Room Wall*

"Greg Cielec is Cleveland's Mark Twain."
Michael Heaton, the *Cleveland Plain Dealer's Minister of Culture*

"*My Cleveland Story* is a shot-and-beer novel, told with warmth, humor, nostalgia and ethnic blue collar rough-and-tumble truth. Goodness lives in this book."

Patricia Wynn Austin, *Columbus Alive*

"Greg has accomplished the impossible, he has written the Great American Novel, the Ohio version. It is wonderful. I absolutely love it, from the characters to the voice it is told in. I love it all, *My Cleveland Story.*"

Steve Mackall, Cleveland born, Los Angeles based movie and television writer and performer.

"I love it. If you didn't live a life like the ones in *My Cleveland Story*, you're in luck. If you did, enjoy the walk down memory lane. Greg hits all the bases in this wonderful story."

Pete Gaughan, *Sun Newspapers*

"My college years have been legitimized in *My Cleveland Story.*"
Patty Harken, *FOX8 TV in Cleveland*

"There were so many times I had to stop reading because there was an image or memory of someone from my Cleveland days milling through my thoughts for the first time in years. Any book that can combine sitting in the bleachers at the old stadium for Tribe games and a recipe for perogies is a great find. *My Cleveland Story* depicts life growing up in the Sixties to the Eighties so clearly that I had to stop and make sure that it wasn't *MY Cleveland Story.*"

Jason P. Skoda, *the Lorain Morning Journal*

"*My Cleveland Story* is an engaging story...the stuff movies are made of..."
Ohioana Quarterly, *the Journal of the Ohioana Library Association*

"*My Cleveland Story* is fast paced entertainment."
Craig Wilson, *The Akron Beacon Journal*

"I loved *My Cleveland Story* and could not put it down. You don't have to be a Clevelander to enjoy *My Cleveland Story*."
Virginia Parobek, *BookLovers*

"*My Cleveland Story* is like The Wonder Years...I found myself laughing, crying, and unable to put it down."
Scoop, *The Blitz* in Columbus, Ohio

"Poetic and heroic, there can never be enough accolades for *My Cleveland Story*. You begin to understand what it felt like to have your first kiss with someone whom you had admired from a distance, or experience the loss of a truly loved one."
Craig J. Heimbuch, *The Avon Lake Press*

"Cielec's coming-of-age story *My Cleveland Story* easily transcends generational boundaries. A tip of the Little King bottle to Cielec."
Courtney Baker, *Spot Magazine*

"What *My Cleveland Story* is really about is large families in warm kitchens, good music, good times and friends who love and lose each other. This book has a heart as big as old Municipal Stadium."
Suzanne DeGaetano, *Events & Reviews*

"I've only recently met Greg Cielec, but I feel I've known him all my life ... *My Cleveland Story* has become something of a cult favorite for thirty something North Coasters. If you grew up in the suburbs during the 1970's and early 80's and had any type of social life, you can relate to *My Cleveland Story*. You might discover a little piece of your own story and meet a new friend along the way."
Joe Stitt, *Sun Newspapers*

"*My Cleveland Story* is a touching look at coming-of-age. To say that you have to be from Ohio to enjoy it is wrong. It is a very emotional ride and well worth it. Even the guys may shed a tear."

Amazon.com

"I picked up *My Cleveland Story* and couldn't put it down until I was finished. The character development was so real, I had to remind myself it was a work of fiction. I felt like I was there, smelling the smells, hearing the music, feeling the emotions, but from a corner in the room. I applaud Greg, and look forward to his next book."

Amazon.com

"In *A Poem on a Bar Room Wall*, Cielec's description of Cleveland neighborhood life is especially rendered...dancing to polka music, working at the West Side Market, eating perogies..."

Akron Beacon Journal

"A Poem on a Bar Room Wall ... has a kind of magic that draws us in and makes us forget time."

Josh Echt, Columbus based writer
Author of Cleveland-based YA novels: *Coach Olivia: An Underdog Story and Me, Maria and the Mother of God.*

"One of the best of the year ... *A Poem on a Bar Room Wall* is a love letter to Cleveland neighborhoods."

Akron Beacon Journal, 2015

"*My Cleveland Story* is the first book I have read since Call of the Wild in Mr. Cielec's ninth grade English class."

Brian Heinzerling

"Thanks for making me a part of *My Cleveland Story*. I really appreciate it."

Michael Stanley, *Cleveland music icon*

"Great job, Dude, on *My Cleveland Story*."

Colin Dussault, *Cleveland's Bluesman*

"*Home and Away Games* is another wonderful story from a master storyteller."

Pete Gaughan, *Sun Newspapers*

"*My Cleveland Story*" is a great book! A fantastic story that follows two best friends, set in Cleveland in "the good ol' days" as well as the two friends' respective college campuses. Paints a vivid picture of growing up: high school football, first loves, graduation, college, returning home. As the author writes, "it was the golden age, before HIV but after crabs."

Matt Perse, English Professor

"As Program Director for my local Kiwanis club, I feel it is necessary to research my speakers. I picked up *My Cleveland Story* and couldn't put it down until I was finished. The character development was so real, I had to remind myself it was a work of fiction. Living near Cleveland I could picture my self at the old stadium watching the Browns, or the Tribe. I think what hit me the most was the music. I grew up on MSB and I could picture my self in college and remembered how important the music was, what I was doing the first time I heard a particlular song, or a specific memory was jarred at the mention of a song. I felt like I was there, smelling the smells, hearing the music, feeling the emotions, but from a corner in the room. I applaud Greg, and look forward to his next book."

Nikki Krejci, Cleveland, Ohio

"I must admit the fact that *My Cleveland Story* made strong mention of MSB, Springsteen, the Browns and the greatest city in the world was my main reason for wanting to read it, and it is heavy on Cleveland details. But to say that you have to be from Ohio to enjoy it is wrong. It is a very emotional ride and well worth it. Even the guys may shed a tear."

Jim Wheeler - Upper Sandusky, Ohio

"Living in the Cleveland area of the 60's-80's, we all remember the Kardiac Kids, Springsteen, Michael Stanley, and our poor Indians who lost game after game. As the Streetsboro High Librarian, I have worked with Greg for several years and I can assure you that he has lived and felt every word of his novel. You too will feel all the ups and downs of his coming of age with his friends Mate and Beth- and you will shed a few tears. Every person with a Cleveland connection should buy this book and relive those "wonderful times."

Mrs. Barbara Jo McKee, Librarian, Streetsboro, Ohio

'*My Cleveland Story* is more than just a great trip down Cleveland's memory lane. What drew me to reading this book more than once was the warmth of the characters. Greg, Mate, and Beth are characters who stay with you long after you have read the book. My favorite excerpts involve the descriptions of Mate's family the Majowski's. They have the kind of home where the door is always open, there's always more than enough food to share, and plenty of good times to be had. The celebration and appreciation of all the simple things in life are apparent in every page."

Christina Conti, Librarian, Akron, Ohio

"In *A Poem on a Bar Room Wall,* The narrator's voice makes it seem like you are sitting on a bar stool—perhaps near the wall with the poem—listening to a man tell his stories. The inclusion of some notable Cleveland landmarks is fun, but these stories can come from anywhere in the USA, so you don't have to be from the North Coast to appreciate them. So kick back with a beer and enjoy protagonist, Jeff Smolinski, as he relates his memories of life, love and family secrets."

Deanna Adams - Author of *Rock 'N' Roll and the Cleveland Connection* and *A Place We Belong*

Other works by Greg Cielec

Fiction

My Cleveland Story (1998)

Home and Away Games (2007)

A Poem on a Bar Room Wall (2015)

Nonfiction

Finding Voice: Poetry from the 2100 Lakeside Men's Shelter (2011) (Editor)

The Brown Jug Cook Book (2013)
(co-author with Ed Wolf and Bill Stroud)

My Rock and Roll Girl

By Greg Cielec

Pink Flamingo Press and Creative Endeavors
Cleveland, Ohio
2025

ISBN 978-0-9665724-8-3

First Editon, Fall 2025

Book Design and Proofreading by David Hostetler

Cover Design by Kristi Gunyula

Pink Flamingo Press and Creative Endeavors
Cleveland, Ohio
2025

To all of the rock and roll girls that have gone through my life, especially Lynn, Kyle, and Carla

Chapter 1

From the first scene of the first episode of *My Rock and Roll Girl.*

Scene One, Episode One, **My Rock and Roll Girl**

Scene: Typical 1970's high school between classes. Kids walking in all directions. The camera zooms in on two young boys, probably freshmen or sophomores. One is handing the other a stack of record albums, the one on the outside is **The Rise and Fall of Ziggy Stardust** by David Bowie and the Spiders from Mars.

CUT TO

BREWSTER (the one handing over the records):
Remember, my brother will kill me if you scratch any of these.

CONNOR
I know, I know. I'll tape them as soon as I get home and get them back to you. I got to run, or I'll be late.

CUT TO

Connor running down the hall to his next class, obviously late. He's just barely able to keep both his books and the record albums under control. He rounds a corner just as he seems to gain control over the books and the records and he runs full blast into Amanda Robinson. The Amanda Robinson, the best-looking girl in the tenth grade. Sister of Annamaria Robinson, the best-looking girl in the senior class (and the whole school), and Alexandra Robinson, the best-looking girl in the freshmen class. Connor's books and records go flying, as does Amanda's books.

AMANDA
Oh my God, I'm sorry.

CONNOR
(making eye contact with her): after a long pause where he just looked in her eyes...
No, no, my fault.

CUT TO
They both start picking up the books and records and then Amanda exclaims...

AMANDA
Oh my God, are you into Bowie? I just love him. Are you going to his show this Thursday? You know he's here, right?

CUT TO
Connor, who was falling in love second by second, wanted the moment to last longer. The bell to start class rings in the background; he ignores it.

CONNOR
I'd love to go to the show this Thursday, but I don't have

the money for things like that.
Plus, it's sold out.

AMANDA
Well this is your lucky day. My sisters and I have two extra tickets. Would you like to come? You can bring a friend.

CONNOR
Are you kidding me?

AMANDA
We had some friends in college who were coming home for the show, but they aren't now.
The tickets are yours if you want them.

CONNOR
How much are they?

AMANDA
Don't worry about that.

CONNOR
OK, I won't worry about that. Can I pay you next week?

AMANDA
(with a smile): We will worry about that next week.

CONNOR
OK, me and my friend Brewster are in.

CUT TO
They pause for a moment, then they both realize they

are late for class.

CONNOR and AMANDA
together: "Oh Shit!"

CUT TO
And he takes off in one direction and she in another.

This story probably begins when we discovered David Bowie when we were in tenth grade. My older brother had his earlier albums, and Dave asked if he could borrow them and make cassette copies.

I handed him the albums outside of my locker and told him, "Remember my brother will kill me if you scratch any of them."

"I know, I know. Tell him I'll bring them by tonight after I'm finished."

He went one way to his math class; I went the other way to my history class. Little did we know how all of our lives were going to change.

As he tried to juggle the albums with his textbooks, Dave momentarily lost track of where he was going and walked straight into Emily Robinson, and his books and my brother's albums went flying.

Before he could say anything Emily said, "Oh my God, I'm sorry." She immediately put her books down and started helping him gather his stuff. Suddenly she became quite animated. "Oh my God, are you into Bowie? Are you going to the show this Thursday? You know he's here."

Before Dave could explain that he had no money and no connections to go to the sold-out show that Thursday at Public Hall, Emily said, "I think my sisters and I have a couple of extra tickets. Would you be interested in going?"

Dave stood there speechless, not knowing what to say. Going to the Bowie show with the Robinson sisters, the Robinson sisters, the thought of it happening left him stunned and stuttering. Finally he gained his composure. "I'd love to go."

Emily took out a pen and wrote her phone number on one of his notebooks. "Here's my phone number, give me a call Wednesday, and we will figure out what we are doing. Let me know if you want to bring a friend."

I had been to a few concerts with my brother and his crew, and my parents made sure we saw at least one professional play a year usually at the Cleveland Play House, but I had never seen a concert that was also a play that told a story like Bowie's Ziggy Stardust show.

It had many of the elements of a play, including make-up and costumes, lighting, characters, and somewhat of a story line. It had all the elements of a concert, including an enthusiastic audience, great musicians starting with Mick Ronson on lead guitar, and awesome songs written and sung by David Bowie. Wow! I was mesmerized by the whole thing, one great song, one great moment after another. Double Wow! "Starman," "Suffragette City," "Ziggy Stardust," plus my other favorite Bowie songs like "Changes" and "Rebel, Rebel."

Being with the girls only made it better. They walked into Public Hall like they owned the place; this definitely wasn't their first rodeo. They had great seats, tenth row from the stage on the floor. The girls seemed to know the people around us.

On the way down we were introduced to Emily's two sisters, Erin who was a senior and Beth who was a freshman. I had seen all of them around school and had immediately put all three of them in the out of my league category. There I found myself sitting with all three of them and a few other friends that were almost as good looking in the tenth row at the hottest show in town. I couldn't keep my eyes off Erin, obviously out of my league.

The trip downtown was just as amazing. When the girls pulled up outside Dave's house to pick us up, it wasn't in any ordinary car. It was a 1970 Cadillac Coup de Ville, robin egg blue in color. "It's our mom's car," Beth said. The girls all broke into a laugh. "We made a deal with her that if we all keep our grades up, we could use it for special occasions like today."

"What's so funny about that?" I asked.

"Well," Emily said, "It just seems between the three of us there seems to be more and more special occasions each week."

It had what at the time was GM's premier stereo package with a cassette deck, white wall tires, and soft brush upholstery. Its back seat was huge, very easily seating four across. It was the bomb.

"We need something to call it. Any suggestions, fellas?" Erin asked. "We haven't seemed to come up with an appropriate one yet."

"Give Mike some time, and he will come up with one," Dave responded. "He's an aspiring writer." I sat there in silence, embarrassed that my best friend shared one of my secrets with people we had really just met. For a moment Erin took her eyes off the road and glanced at me with what appeared to be a touch of respect.

"Well, that's one of our chores for the next month or two, is to come up with a nickname for this beautiful beast." It would be Dave, not me, that would soon come up with the appropriate name.

To and back to the show I sat in front between Erin and Beth. Erin was totally out of my league, the best looking senior in the school. I would soon find out she was also the coolest. Being protective of her younger sisters, she had the self-confidence I had never seen in a girl before. Yet she didn't talk down to any of us, and treated us all as equals. Too bad she was so totally out of my league; I could fall in love with her.

None of the sisters wore much make up if any at all. However, they all wore a touch of the same perfume; years later I would find out it was called Diane von Furstenberg.

For most of the time in the car I conversed with Beth who was sitting to my right. She was only a freshman, but she possessed a bit of the self confidence that her older sisters had. She also possessed something. I've never really been able to pinpoint exactly what it was, but it made guys slightly afraid of her. Little did I know the small talk we made on the way to and back from that show would be the beginning of the most unique friendship I would have in my life.

So I went to the David Bowie show with three beautiful sisters and a few of their friends, singing and laughing and enjoying every second. Dave and Emily just sat next to each other, still holding hands, and seeming to enjoy the moment also.

After the show as we headed out of downtown with Erin still behind the wheel, she skipped getting on either freeway back to our neck of the woods. Instead, she hopped on the Lorain Carnegie Bridge and headed due west up Lorain Avenue. In what could only be described as a shady neighborhood, we pulled up to a lit store front that had two neon signs, one saying Steve's Lunch; the other saying Hot Dogs. And as much as the concert was unforgettable, our first trip to Steve's Lunch afterward was just as memorable.

You walked in off Lorain and there were maybe ten stools across the counter and five or six tables against the wall. Menu on the wall featuring dozens of items, but no one I ever knew got anything but hot dogs when there, either Slaw Dogs or Steve's Dogs. I can't remember which one was which, but they were covered with chili, onions, and cheddar cheese. Then, of course, you would lather them with mustard.

They had these overweight older women in spandex pants behind the counter, and this very old guy, who had to be in his eighties, working the kitchen. They would yell his name each time they needed an order of French fries…"Pete, Pete!!!" they would scream. We would order extra fries halfway through our meals just to be treated to this. After a night out drinking, or at a ball game or concert, nothing was better than stopping at Steve's.

The clientele was something else. Kids like us, who were coming home from someplace like concerts and house parties and bars, workers getting off their shifts, bums looking for a free meal, lonely men nursing a cup of coffee with no place else to go, cops and cabbies and off shift strippers and ladies of the evening were all represented. Over the years we would go to Steve's Lunch dozens of times and it seemed something always happened. One time some bum pulled a knife on us, and we all broke out laughing. The poor guy was so embarrassed it looked like he was holding back tears.

The place always smelled like Steve's. It smelled of smoke, grease, bad pot, and perfume worn by the strippers, who came in for a cup of coffee during their breaks.

Our first night there was overwhelming, even after the show we had just seen. We were sitting on stools at the counter with Elizabeth sitting on my lap and Emily sitting on Dave's. We were taking it all in when one the waitresses barked at us, "What will you have?"

Dave looked at me, then looked at her and said, "Give us your two biggest prime ribs and two bottles of Lowenbrau."

The waitress looked like she was going to punch Dave; luckily, Erin stepped in. "We will each have two slaw dogs a piece, French fries, and cokes." She wrote the order down then yelled at the top of her voice, "Pete, Pete, seven French fries."

If the place wasn't cool enough the juke box played old school rock and roll from consoles sitting on the counter. Elvis, BB King, Etta James, Bobby Darin, Dion, Ella…priceless music in a priceless establishment. When bands still made 45s, it was considered a medal of honor for local bands if their 45 made it on the juke box at Steve's.

That night of the Bowie concert was the first of dozens of trips to Steve's Lunch. When coming home from downtown, Steve's became our after-hours joint from then on.

Years later when it went up in a flash because of a grease fire in the kitchen, it was the lead story on all four local 11:00 newscasts and front-page news the next day.

Erin pulled up in front of Dave's house to let us out. I lived right around the corner and could walk home from there. I was busy hugging Erin, Beth, and the other girls goodbye. I hugged all of them at least twice, didn't want the night to end. With four people sitting in the back seat, Emily was partially sitting on Dave's lap. They were still holding hands and were oblivious to the noise and commotion around them, and Dave did not notice that we were parked in front of his house.

"That was probably the single best time of my life," Dave said to her.

"What's this probable stuff? Let's make it the absolute best time," Emily replied by putting her arms around him and giving him a big, wet, lasting kiss upon his lips. To say he was enjoying the moment was an understatement. It probably would have gone on for hours if not for Erin getting impatient and wanting to get home. She honked the horn and said, "You two, go get a hotel room." At the time she was the only one of us who got the joke.

Yes, it was quite a night that first night out with the sisters. We had no idea then how many great nights (and days!) would be in our future.

By the time I got to my house it was later than any time ever on a school night. As I snuck in the back door trying not to make too much noise, I was greeted by my mother sitting at the kitchen table drinking a cup of coffee. She or my dad always waited up until we were all home and in bed, every night, no matter what.

Just as I was about to beg for forgiveness, I noticed she had a slight smile on her face. I paused for a moment, not sure what to say.

"You have a glow to you right now that I have never seen before," she said. She patiently waited for me to reply, and after a few awkward moments of silence, I just opened up. I told her everything…about the girls and how cool they were…the car…and how great David Bowie was…the seats we sat in…and our trip to Steve's afterward. I talked to her more that night than I ever did before about anything. She just sat there and listened, taking it all in. Finally, when I ran out of things to tell her, she got up, came over to where I was sitting, gave me a hug and kissed me on top of my head. "My youngest boy is becoming a young man," she said. I looked up and thought I saw a tear rolling down her cheek. She walked down the hallway to her and my dad's bedroom, and I went upstairs to mine.

On the way to school the next morning on the bus (yes, we were still loser underclassmen without our own cars), Dave and I couldn't get over all that had happened the night before. Both of us were so excited that neither of us got much sleep. Since neither of us had Emily in a class or lunch period that semester, we decided if either of us ran into her over the course of the day, we'd find out what we owed her for the tickets and if we could pay her next week. Still not believing our luck in the whole thing, we wondered who the tickets were originally for. They must have been meant for someone.

I was the first to encounter Emily between classes. "Great time last night; we really appreciated it."

"No problem," she replied. "We were happy to have you aboard."

"What do we owe you for tickets? Dave and I can pay you next week."

Emily paused with a slight grin on her face. "You don't owe us for anything. The tickets were free."

"Free? In the tenth row?"

She just smiled. "You don't know who our dad is, do you? He's president of Local Union 245. He can, and does, gets us tickets to almost anything. You can thank him when you meet him."

"Wow, that's great."

Just as we were going to walk off in different directions to different classes, I turned and asked her one more question. "Hey, we were wondering, why us? Those tickets had to be originally for someone else."

She stopped and said something very matter of factly. "They were originally meant for my old boyfriend who goes to college at Kent. He's been drinking himself into a stupor every day since he went away, and he is no longer part of my life anymore. When we got the tickets, he was, but now he ain't."

The Bowie concert was the beginning of Dave and Emily's relationship, for the lack of a better term. It was the most mature high school romance I had ever seen. High school is filled with a lot of drama, and most high school relationships are filled with even more drama. You didn't call; you didn't meet me after class; I saw you talking to so and so, and on and on…

I was a typical teenager, or so I thought. I had dated a few girls during those years; and, of course, I was soon to start my unique relationship with Beth. Nothing ever went smoothly.

Dave and Emily's relationship was never like everyone else's. Everyone I knew, both boys and girls (and a few parents) were jealous of their relationship. It was so un-teenager. Until our senior year when Emily and Beth completely took over possession of the car from their mom, Dave and Emily did not ride to school together. Most of the high school years they didn't eat lunch together or meet up between classes. If they went a whole day at school not seeing each other, it was no big deal. They spent little time talking with each other on the phone. One night of the weekend was reserved for doing something with a group of friends, sometimes including both of them. One night a weekend they usually did something together, even if it was just hanging out at either of their houses and watching television. Concerts were usually a group effort and included Beth's sisters.

But when they were together, they seemed very compatible. They laughed at the same things, shared stupid jokes with each other, and usually liked the same books, movies, and bands.

They took it slowly but sooner or later the sex thing kept appearing. It was two months to the day of the Bowie show that brought us all together. They were wrestling with each other on the couch in her parent's basement.

Dave looked her in the eyes and said, "I got the feeling that one day soon, maybe even today, we will find out what all the hub bub is about sex. But I got to tell you, I'm slightly scared. I've never done it."

"Neither have I," she responded.

"Not even with Tommy Witham?" He was Emily's old boyfriend now off at college.

"I didn't do any of this stuff with him."

And so on the couch in her parents' basement on a cold Thursday night over Christmas break, with Led Zeppelin IV playing on the stereo, Dave and Emily had for the first time, but surely not the last, become, as they called it in our health classes, "sexually active."

They held on to each other in silence when they finished; they had both seemed to enjoy it.

"Wow, that was something," Emily said.

Erin sensed that Emily and Dave's relationship was headed in that direction and knew what to do. In those days there was a lot of denial by parents about their children's sex lives. I'm not sure for some parents it has changed much over the years. Most parents just couldn't picture their son or daughter having sex, and if they knew about it, they usually just ignored it.

Back in the '70s the Free Clinic was really the only place young women could get birth control without their parent's permission. Located in a store front over in University Circle, Erin first heard about it from some girls she knew from the local music scene. When she sensed that her younger sisters were about to cross the sexual line, she took them to the clinic.

Beth protested. This was before our first back of the Caddy moment.

"Believe me," Erin said. "You guys are not that far off. And if any of the three of us ever got pregnant, it would be all three of us catching hell from Mom and Dad."

Beth started showing a bit of jealously towards her older sisters when she realized they were both having sex with their boyfriends. Emily had Dave, and Erin always had a boyfriend or two chasing her. Up until then Beth had never had sex, and she had never had a serious boyfriend. Her older sisters kept telling her it was no big deal, that her time would come. She felt they were treating her like a little girl instead of a high school freshman.

We had been flirting with each other since that first night at the Bowie concert. Well, at least I had been flirting with her; she had shown much disinterest towards me. As we spent more time with each other, mostly in a group that included her sisters, Dave, and other assorted friends, she started treating me more as a close friend and not as a romantic interest. She had a front row seat watching her sisters get more involved with their boyfriends.

"I am not like them," she told me. "I am not going to spend my high school years looking for a boyfriend."

Even though she was the youngest, she had bigger plans for her future than her older sisters. "My life is not going to be getting a job out of high school, finding a husband, buying a house in Parma, and having three kids before I'm 25. I want more than that."

As I got to know her better I really started to like her sense of humor. All three sisters were funny to a degree, but her humor was sharper and more observant. She had nicknames for everyone. When her sisters got new hairdos based on the characters from Charley's Angels, they became Farrah 1 and Farrah 2. When their mom hired a once-a-week cleaning service to do housework, she became HOY, Homemaker of the Year. She called her dad (but not to his face) the Don, after Don Corleone from *The Godfather*, the man with all the connections.

It was late in the first spring, and we were hanging together on a Sunday afternoon. Their family was having friends over for a cookout to celebrate opening of their pool for the summer.

Beth and I were sitting at a patio table with her mom. Beth had been moody; I knew something was on her mind.

Her mother turned towards us and said, "Would you two kids go out to my car and get the pop and beer that is in the trunk and put some in the coolers by the pool and the rest in the downstairs refrigerator?"

We got up and walked outside towards the blue Cadillac, which was still technically their mom's car even though the girls had pretty much taken it over. We were walking along the passenger side on our way to the trunk when suddenly in one quick move Beth opened the back door and tackled me into the back seat.

A lot of things happened quickly. I remember locking lips, and her hands in my shorts and my hands in hers. Then we were both out of our shorts, and then I was inside of her. It felt great; it was awesome, and it was over before you knew it. She then looked me in the eyes and said, "God, was that great. Have you ever done that before?"

"No," I replied.

"Me neither."

The next thing you know we were back in our clothes and taking the pop and beer in. Five minutes later we were sitting with her mom again talking about nothing in particular. It was months before we would have another moment together, and years before we talked about what happened in the backseat.

Little did I know that later that week I would have another landmark high school moment.

Like all the other fun times in my life, the high school years were over way too quickly. It was four years of friends and concerts and sports and dances. We had not only a good group of friends, but also for the most part good teachers and coaches and supportive parents. Dave and I played two sports, although we weren't very good in either of them, took turns being class president, and, of course, hung around with the best clique of girls in the school.

One great thing that happened to us was that Emily's mom and dad really liked us. And that led to Big Ed arranging for our summer and after school jobs. Since he was president of a union local, it was always a union job. That meant that when most of our classmates were making minimum wage at a fast-food joint or at a store at the mall, we were making 5 times that as union janitors, delivery guys, or running a punch press in a machine shop.

Once we hooked up with Emily and her sisters they pretty much ran our social lives, and that was great. There always seemed something was going on; and if there wasn't, they would make it happen.

The sisters and their crew were responsible for our finest all-time athletic moment, a legendary event still talked about today. The spring of our sophomore year our baseball team got on an unusual winning streak. In northern states like Ohio the state baseball tournament overlaps with the regular season. We had a pretty decent team, but couldn't put together any sort of winning streak except when we played a state playoff game. We could not lose. We would lose two conference games but then play a playoff game, and we would win it. That started in the sectionals, took us through the districts, and suddenly we found ourselves in the regionals, the sweet sixteen. We were the only team left that had a losing record, and that found us playing the number one seed in the state, one of the all-boys Catholic schools. They had a scholarship athlete at almost every position, and their only losses were on their spring training trip to Florida. Now every high school team seems to go on a spring training trip, but back then it was pretty rare.

Our school always had a chip on its shoulder whenever we played one of the bigger schools in our league or one of the Catholic all-boys schools. We just found ourselves overly matched too often.

The day of the game was unseasonably warm; early May felt like the Fourth of July. When I sat down for lunch, I could tell something was up.

"You got that look in your eyes. What's up?" I said to Emily. "What are you planning?" The girls at our table all started to smile and look at each other.

"We have been worrying all week about how we could support you guys in your big game against the mighty Saints."

One of the other girls chimed in. "But then we thought about those poor souls on the other team...stuck in class all day...no girlfriends or no girls period in sight."

"Why are you worried about them? What about us? We need all the help we can get."

Emily leaned over and kissed me very sisterly on the cheek. "Don't worry my friend, as they say in baseball lingo, we have all the bases covered."

Just then Dave appeared and sensed something amiss. "You two aren't running off and getting married, are you?"

"Nope," said Emily. "But when that happens you will be the first to know."

They were the higher seed; but since we had our own on campus field, we got to host the game. In fact, we had a pretty good field that butted up next to a city park. Behind home plate there was seating for around 200, and we had built in dugouts. Down both foul lines and across the outfield fence parents, classmates, friends, and fans would bring lawn furniture and sit and watch the game.

We usually didn't have a big crowd. But that particular day we were playing one of the big boys; it was a regional game, and with the summer-like weather we had more than the usual number of fans. The fact that the outfield fence separated the school property from the city park would soon come into play.

I would later find out that most of the planning traced back to Erin, with both of her younger sisters helping with the implementation. Erin was a very independent and mobile young lady for a senior in high school. She could be seen at every concert, school or CYO dance on our side of town, and, of course, had been hanging around the 18 and over music clubs since she was 16. She was simply dynamite, and both of her younger sisters owed much of their personalities and styles to her.

It seemed like Erin had a boyfriend at every other high school. In truth it usually went this way; she'd meet someone, he would ask her out; they would go on a date or two, and then she'd end it out of boredom. Instead of going to a movie and out for a pizza with these dates, she much preferred a night out with her crowd, at a show or a dance or a club. Dating bored her; a night out with laughter and dancing and singing was what she liked.

Because of that Erin had no use for the boys who went to the all-boys schools splattered around the city. She had been on too many lousy dates with them. They had no skills on how to treat a girl right, and all they wanted to talk about was their schools and their sports. Their dispositions were stuck somewhere in the '50s.

Almost everything the girls had planned went off perfectly. In the city park right outside the centerfield fence they set up as their home base. Already there were a couple of volleyball courts, picnic tables, and swings. Twenty or so of the girls arrived about 45 minutes before the game, even before our opponents who had to fight crosstown traffic. Since it was the first hot day of the year, the girls came dressed ready to go to the beach. Swimsuits, bikinis, haltertops, and Hawaiian shirts were in abundance. They brought beach balls and frisbees, as well as a giant boombox which played our version of beach music, i.e., the Beach Boys, the Lovin' Spoonful, Bob Marley, and that new guy who sang about Bloody Marys and Margaritas, Jimmy Buffett.

The girls made sure the place smelled like a beach, with each of them wearing an overabundance of suntan lotion loaded with coconut oil. I didn't even know until later that a couple of the girls snuck on the field before school was out and coated the bases and the pitching rubber with coconut oil. It wasn't just the outfield that smelled like a beach. Each of the girls was also wearing bright red lipstick.

When our opponents arrived, they parked their bus in the lot north of where the girls were set up, and they literally had to walk through the middle of all of it to get to the field. They got their eyes filled with legs and breasts and big hair and red lipstick showing sexy smiles, and whatever mind set they had on the game got broken.

When it got to be game time, their minds were someplace else. The best team in the state would go the first three innings without getting a hit and commit six errors in the field. We would score three unearned runs and go into the fourth leading 3-0.

They tried to come back but just couldn't make it happen. Anytime they seemed to be getting some momentum a beach ball or frisbee would fly onto the field from the park in centerfield, and play would have to be delayed. The longer the game went the more girls in swimsuits were showing up in the outfield. The music kept getting slightly louder inning by inning, and the kids in the outfield were definitely having too good of a time. Since the park in centerfield was city property and not on school property, there was nothing any administrator, coach, or umpire could do about it.

For big games we would often use girls from the softball team as ball girls in left and right field. Erin made sure it was the two most voluptuous girls on the team, Abbie Bennett and her own sister Beth. Instead of wearing their softball uniforms Erin found a couple of old baseball uniforms that buttoned up the front and were a bit too small for both girls. Their jobs were to distract the left and right fielders, as well as the third and first basemen. Let's just say they accomplished their mission.

Our JV season had ended weeks earlier, and Dave and I were brought up to fill the last two spots on the varsity. We were lousy hitters but were both pretty good in the field. We got to play more than we thought we would; it was mostly garbage time, but we enjoyed being around the older jocks, and the coaches did a great job of making us feel at home. We did not expect to play in the big game.

The crowd at the game kept getting bigger and bigger. I remember their coaches in between innings telling their players to "get your heads in the game."

But it never happened. We scored two more runs, both unearned on errors, and were leading 5-0 going into the last inning. Even though the game was at our field, they were the higher seed and got to bat last. We scored our last run on a wild throw to home plate as one of their outfielders flubbed another ball. There was a collision between the runner and the catcher, but our guy was safe by a mile. Our guy slid in headfirst and cut his forehead open on the collision. It was one of those cuts that looked worse than it was, a lot of blood for a not so deep wound. However, more importantly, he was our right fielder, and he needed a replacement. How do you think I felt when I heard my name called by our coach, "Mike, get in the game." There I was having a grand time sitting on the end of the bench enjoying the game with the other scrubs and the next thing I know I'm out there in right field warming up with the ball girl who happened to be Beth.

I was scared to death. I had never been in that type of situation in a varsity game before, let alone a regional game against the best team in the state. Every time a new batter came to bat, I heard myself saying, don't hit it to me, don't hit it to me.

Maybe they finally got their composure, maybe they finally realized the dire situation they were in; but they scored three quick runs, and we managed a couple of outs. We went through every pitcher on our staff.

We were leading 5-3. They had the bases loaded, bottom of the last inning, with one of their studs up to bat. I'm out in right field crapping my pants. They had yet to hit a ball my way, and I just wanted it to stay that way. There were two out. All we needed was one more out.

Right-handed batter who had pulled everything to left field so far. He was down in the count 1-2. And then it happened.

Our pitcher threw a fast ball outside, hoping he would chase it, which he did. However, instead of swinging and missing he got a piece of it and sent it hurling down the right field line. The runners were all going with the pitch, and it was uncertain whether it was going to land fair or foul.

I did not hesitate; I took off as fast as I could, running to where

I thought the ball was going to land. I was running as fast as I could which really wasn't that fast. I had a good eye on the ball, and it seemed like it was going to drop in front of me just inside the foul line. I ran, I ran, then I dove and extended my body as far as I could. Just as I was going to hit the ground, with my glove extended on my right hand, I felt the thud of the ball. I had made the impossible catch to end the game! I rolled over once, then stood up holding the glove above my head for the world to see the ball inside of it.

I really didn't need to do that because within seconds I was mobbed by the complete team and most of the girls from centerfield. My teammates were pounding on me, and I didn't care. The girls kissed me all over my face, and it was covered with red lipstick. And again, I didn't care. Tears were rolling down my face. The only person with more tears running down her face than me was my mom, who grabbed me and hugged me on my way out to the centerfield celebration. I wanted the moment to never end.

The front page of the old *Cleveland Press* sports page the next day had a photo of the pile of people on top of me with the headline "Miracle Catch wins big upset." My parents had that photo mounted and framed and on the wall in their living room for the rest of their lives.

I remember Erin and Emily invited everyone over to their house for swimming afterward, and Big Ed and Barb cooked hamburgers and dogs on the grill, and it seemed everyone there came up and told me about their perspective on the catch. Most said they thought there was going to be no way I would catch it, and they would win the game. "Ye of little faith," I responded.

Two days later we would lose the regional final in eleven innings 3-2. We were disappointed, but we also had our once in a lifetime win in our back pockets.

Since our social lives changed drastically after meeting the sisters, and since their father was responsible for the Bowie tickets, we decided we needed to do something in return. It started with the Bowie tickets, then there were other concerts and ball games and even a loge for a Browns game.

This was years before we realized that Big Ed was one of the guys that was in on it. It was an unregulated string of politicians, gangsters, union officials, and businessmen who ran most of what went on in the city. Everything from major building projects to government contracts went through them. But we didn't know it back then.

We had no idea. To us he was the greatest guy in the world. Simply because we were friends with his daughters, who by the way loved him beyond explanation, he took a liking to us. At first we felt guilty about all the free stuff. The Sunday morning after the Bowie show, Dave and I went over to their house and raked all their leaves and gave the lawn one last cutting before winter set in. A month later when we had our first snow fall we got up early before school and shoveled their driveway. All through the rest of our high school days, we kept doing those things. We both learned also to clean their pool.

That first spring he asked us if we would help him clean out their garage and, of course, we said yes. We spent the day moving boxes, scrubbing walls and the floor, and cleaning out closets. Afterward we sat around a table by their pool as Big Barb served us lunch.

"I want to tell you guys something," Ed said as we munched on ham and cheese sandwiches. "I really appreciate you guys being friends with our daughters. We know they are in safe hands, and you will always look out for them."

We didn't know what to say. Big Ed continued, "The girls tell me you both turned 16." He paused for a moment and took two business cards out of his wallet. "Drop by my office when there are a couple of weeks of school left. I'll set you up with summer jobs, good jobs where you won't be making minimum wage."

Big Ed was a robust man, burly, looked a lot like the guys he represented, guys used to working with their hands through summer heat and winter cold. He came up through the union's rank until he became the onsite representative for almost any job he was on. He had a good ear to listen to anyone's complaints or problems and was just as good at resolving conflicts. After years of having political figureheads at the head of the union's local, when the local's presidency became open, he ran and easily won. The guys on the jobs were happy to have one of their own running the union.

You could see where the girls got their beauty when you got to know their mom, Barb. She was a middle age version of her daughters, and I always assumed she was a beauty in her younger years. She was the daughter of an Irish steel worker whom she loved tremendously and found in Big Ed a man who reminded her of her father. She was very content, being the wife of a union official and the mother of three beautiful girls.

Big Ed's father and mother came over in the '30s when things in Europe were getting strange. For the first ten years they kept their name from the old country, but it was one of those Eastern European names that no one could pronounce or spell. He wanted to Americanize it and took a name everyone knew, Robinson, after the great ball player Jackie Robinson.

And Big Ed and Barb loved Dave and me. I guess we were the sons they never had.

From the time we hooked up with the girls, until the time we graduated, high school flew by. Looking back on all those years makes it seem it was just moments that too soon disappeared. Dave and I, as well as the girls, knew the big secret of being happy in high school, get the best grades possible and avoid the stupid stuff. Don't come late to school or to class; be polite to teachers and coaches even if you don't like them; get assignments done on time; and stay active in and out of school. Most of us "good kids" understood this from ninth grade on. At home and at school, I soon realized the better my grades, and the more I got involved in activities, the more freedom

I got.

And neither Dave nor I were hounded about what our careers were to be. It was first get through high school with the goal of getting into a good college. I always wanted to be a writer; my family and close friends always knew that, but Dave was in an awkward situation. Emily and I were probably the only ones who knew what Dave really wanted as a career, and that was to become a teacher like his father.

But there was a problem. At the time we were coming of age and trying to figure out what we wanted out of life, teaching was a dying profession. No one was going into teaching.

This was complicated by the experiences of Dave's father. He was a junior high science teacher at one of the west side Cleveland junior highs. The school was in an older, still mostly white neighborhood. When we were younger, he loved his job. He loved his job until bussing came and tore the city's schools apart.

Much has been researched and written about the bussing that was implemented in northern cities like Cleveland, Detroit, and Boston, especially how it affected the students and the neighborhoods. But very little was researched and written about the affect bussing had on the teachers and their families who were left to deal with the mess that appeared in their classrooms.

Dave's dad went from an always happy guy who was always smiling to a bitter person who spent his last teaching years counting the days until he retired. Every day became a battle with his classes half filled with kids who spent every morning on a school bus fighting through rush hour for 45 minutes to go to a school miles away from their neighborhoods and the schools they had attended the year before. And so, he would tell his children under no circumstances were they to go into education.

That's not to say we were completely angels. At that time, it was so easy to get an I.D. to get in the 18 and over music clubs. There weren't pictures on the driving licenses yet, so one thing you could do is get an older friend or brother to go to the license bureau and say that he had lost his driver's license. He'd show his birth certificate, and they would make him a new one. You would pay the fee and get the old license. The girls looked so much alike that at first Beth or Emily would borrow Erin's license. Since we all started to go out to clubs together, we did the lost license thing or to where they would make you an illegal out of state license. Back then none of this was that hard.

At these clubs we would drink beer. We weren't big beer drinkers, but it helped us to come out of our shells a bit. By the time we were juniors all of our parents would let us grab a beer after mowing the lawn or shoveling the drive, or to watch a ballgame on TV. We also had a get out of jail card that I don't ever remember using, but I think we did. The hotshots in Big Ed's union had a car service they could call 24 hours a day if they needed a ride to the airport, or more importantly, if they needed a ride home at 3:00 after a night of boozing. All five of us had that phone number in our wallets.

Those high school years were, of course, highlighted by the concerts we all went to together. We saw Elton John as the first rock act at the old Coliseum in Richfield. We saw Fleetwood Mac and the Eagles first large halls shows. After we went to that first Bowie show, we went to another one at Public Hall, Golden Earring opening for Bachman Turner Overdrive. My ears hurt for a week. Bob Seger came down from Detroit and played Cleveland so many times that most of us assumed he was from here. And, of course, we saw dozens of MSB shows. Those were the days!

Maybe the coolest things we got to do because of the girls (and their dad!) was going to concerts at the old stadium and sitting in a loge. There were a dozen or so concerts during our high school and college days. They were called the World Series of Rock. Being able to sit in a loge with its own bathroom, plus having food and beverages catered, was luxury beyond our pay grade. I remember seeing everyone from the Stones to Santana to the Beach Boys, all in total comfort.

And as teenagers, we were all also trying to deal with the sex and relationship things. As Jimmy Buffett would say years later, we all wanted relationships; but once we had one, we didn't know what to do with it. To paraphrase that great American poet Bob Seger, we were all working on too many mysteries with no clues at all.

And Big Ed kept to his promise and got the two of us great jobs each summer, always as a union member. We started out sweeping and scrubbing floors, but as people got to know us they started to request us. We would also do some sort of office work. We were making so much more money than our friends from school who were working fast food or at the mall it was embarrassing.

Big Ed and Big Barb treated us as the sons they never had. My parents and Dave's liked the girls' parents because of the jobs we got over breaks, and, of course, they just loved the girls. We were constantly in and out of each other's houses, and never had to knock.

So, you could say high school played out pretty well for us. It was a world filled with concerts and ball games, family outings and picnics, swim parties and Friday night football games. And like all good times in life, it was over before we knew it.

The summer between our junior and senior years, because we had really good grades and were president and vice president of our class, Dave and I got invited to go on one of those college tours to New England and back. We were gone for a week and viewed two colleges a day. They all seemed to blend together, but on our last day on the road we visited the College of the Finger Lakes, a small liberal arts school in upstate New York. As we walked around the campus, something happened to Dave. He later told me that as soon as we stepped on the campus that this was the one. It was a good-looking campus, and I could see him fitting in. Later that fall he went for an overnight visit, and he felt the same when he came back.

A similar thing happened to me. I told our guidance counselor how we enjoyed our trip out east, but that most of those schools were too far from home for me. He mentioned to me that there was a cluster of small colleges in central Ohio that had that New England/Ivy League feel to them. I arranged to go on a trip to visit two of them, one in the morning and the other in the afternoon.

They were both great. The one in the morning had more of an east coast vibe to it, maybe a little too preppy for me. The other one got me the minute I got out of my mom's car and walked into the admissions office. The counselor was also a student who would turn out to be one of my best friends the next year. He took me around the campus, and I kept falling more in love with the place. At the end of the tour, he turned towards me and said, "Do you really have to go home now? Why don't you spend the night? You can crash in my fraternity. We're having a cookout with our little sisters, and you will get to meet a lot of cool people." I made a call home and the next thing I knew I'm playing in a coed touch football game with a bunch of kids on the lawn in front of the fraternity house. Everyone was so nice to me, and I fell in love with each of the girls. They had a fire going on, and a keg of beer tapped on their front porch. This is how I always envisioned college, I said to myself.

I was waiting to get a beer when the girl in front of me turned and started filling my cup. "So, you thinking about joining us here next year?"

"Yes, I am," stumbled out of my mouth.

"Well, I'll tell you one thing; I've never regretted it for a moment," and she turned and ran back to the game, not spilling a drop of her beer. It was on that beautiful fall afternoon, that I decided my college choice. And I never regretted it for a moment.

Financially college was a different game back then. Until they make college once again affordable for everyone, and a life experience first and a career path second, things will remain screwed up. But back in our youth it wasn't like it is today.

Dave and I were both in good financial shape for college. First of all, we weren't from affluent families; and our financial aid forms showed that. We also had great grades and very good test scores; and those both helped a lot.

Between scholarships, grants, and a small loan, my school was very affordable. Once I got my financial aid package I sent the deposit in and never looked anywhere else. I had already saved a lot from the various jobs Big Ed got me; and if I kept on getting them through college breaks, I would be in good shape.

Dave's path was a little different and had several major twists and turns. He had his heart set on Finger Lakes. He really got excited when they told him they were a McKenzie Scholarship school. A McKenzie covered everything from tuition, room and board, and spending money. Those that were a McKenzie school only had one scholarship per class. The admission counselor at Finger Lakes thought he had a really good shot at it. Without it he still would have done well in the financial aid and scholarship department, but it would've included a small loan each year. And that was the only stipulation he had from his parents, no college loans no matter how small.

Dave and I had a great back up, but I didn't need to pursue it. Since we had been working at least during breaks for the union, we were eligible for one of the union's annual scholarships. All Dave had to do was apply, and he got one. It included all tuition, books and expenses, and some spending money for transportation. Because one of the stipulations of the scholarship was you had to attend a four-year public college in the county, and the only one in Cuyahoga County was Cleveland State. So, if he went with the union scholarship, he would be staying at home for school.

Dave wasn't worried about that. He was so sure he was going to get the McKenzie at Finger Lakes that he filed all the paperwork for the union scholarship, thinking he was doing that just to please his parents. He told them if he didn't get the McKenzie to Finger Lakes, he would stay at home and attend Cleveland State. Now Cleveland State today is a pretty vibrant campus with buildings and dorms stretching from Play House Square until Midtown. Back then it was total commuter with nothing but ugly buildings and parking lots. But it was a good school, and if you got to go there free on the union's dime that wasn't so bad. He was so sure he was going to get the McKenzie. He was valedictorian, class president, had done a lot of charity work, had great recommendations from our teachers and some of the people we had worked for. He thought he was a lock.

When the letter came in late May that he didn't get the McKenzie, it took him by surprise. They did offer him their best in house scholarship, but that came along with a stipulation he take a small loan each year. He knew his parents wouldn't be for it. Plus, his parents knew what a great deal the union scholarship was.

For most of the summer missing out on the McKenzie didn't seem to bother him. He prepped as if he was going to CSU, looking for a good used car to buy, lining up a union office job to work part time, even checking into working at the Agora one or two nights a week. Emily was ecstatic he was staying home but didn't really show it. She knew how disappointing not going to Finger Lakes was to him.

We had a great summer. I remember the last concert we all went to before I left for school was America at Blossom, with John Sebastian from the Lovin' Spoonful opening up. From that night on I started to call Beth "Sister Golden Hair." On the way home that night, while they were wrestling around in the back seat, Dave whispered in Emily's ear, "You are my rock and roll girl."

Erin heard just enough of it and asked, "What did you just say?"

And Dave replied, "My rock and roll girl."

"That's it!" Erin exclaimed. "My rock and roll girl."

"Who? Emily?"

"Well, she might be your rock and roll girl, but that's what we are going to call the car from now on, My Rock and Roll Girl!"

And Emily became Dave's rock and roll girl, and the car became the Rock and Roll Girl to all of us.

Emily took a black felt tip pen and along the top edge of the door on the driver's side, along the window edge, she wrote My Rock and

Roll Girl.

After that we had one more Thursday night out together before my parents took me to school Friday morning. I planned on walking over to Dave's house, and the girls were going to pick us up there. Even Erin was coming for our last night together until Christmas break. I walked into his kitchen like I had done hundreds of times before, but I could tell the conversation he was having with his parents was important. At first I thought something bad had happened to someone we knew, but actually it was to a just graduated senior from a high school in Vermont.

"What's up?" I said.

"You won't believe what happened. The kid who beat me out for the McKenzie got in a serious car accident last week. He's going to be laid up for a while, so he isn't going to school this quarter." At first I did not get the connection.

"The college just called; the scholarship is mine, if I still want it. I just have to decide by tomorrow."

His parents knew how much Dave wanted to go away to Finger Lakes, and especially how he moped around the house the last several weeks as friends and classmates had been getting ready to go away. His parents knew, and I knew, and most importantly, Dave knew what his decision was going to be.

Later that night, at Steve's Lunch on Lorain Avenue, after the bars closed, amongst a full house of more than a few over-served partiers munching on slaw dogs, there were several serious conversations going on. The more serious of the two took place in the back seat of a '70 Caddy parked out front.

Dave was going through with Emily what had happened over the last 48 hours with his McKenzie Scholarship. He told her about the other student's accident; he was the kid who beat him out originally, and how he had until tomorrow morning to accept the scholarship, or it would go to the next person on the list.

"I appreciate all your dad has done for me; and I appreciate receiving the union's scholarship, but my dream has always been to go away to college. You know, live in a dorm, meet other people, people from other places. There is nothing wrong with going to CSU; I would've really enjoyed it, and I would meet new people, but they would be like you and me. This is my chance to see the world."

"I guess I'm just in shock. I thought everything was settled. I was looking forward to having you around."

"It was settled then things changed. Sometimes stuff happens."

"You know I would never hold you back."

"And you're not. Listen, I'll be back every summer and every Christmas. You can come and visit."

"I know, I know," she said as she wiped away a tear or two. There was a silent pause of several moments, then she decided to change her disposition. "Well, why all the sadness. We should be celebrating. Do you agree?"

"Yes."

"Well, I can't think of a better thing to do right now…" as she wrapped her arms around him and their lips met and passion filled the backseat once more.

The other conversation was between me and Beth at the counter.

"Don't expect me to write you at school," she said quite earnestly as we sat at the counter waiting for our Slaw Dogs and French fries. "I'm going to be back here, enjoying my senior year and having a good time."

"I don't doubt it. You will be welcome to visit whenever you want."

"I'm going to spend my senior year flirting with every guy I meet and not taking any of them too serious."

"That sounds like you."

"I have to ask you one thing. Have you done the you know what since our moment in the backseat of the car?"

I hesitated, not expecting such a question. She completely ignored me and our moment together for months, then years, and now she brings it up the night before I'm going away to college?

"Have you done it with anyone since then? And don't lie to me. I know you were Abbie Bennett's prom date, and she has had sex with every guy she has dated. She wasn't going to pass up getting laid on her prom night."

I didn't first admit to doing the deed, which I did; and then realized, she knew I did.

"How did you know about that?" I responded with a touch of surprise in my voice.

"Because Abbie is worse than a guy. Every time Abbie has a sexual moment she has to tell the whole softball team. Like I said, worse than a guy."

"Did she say that I was wonderful, romantic, special?" To be honest, it wasn't good at all. Abby was bombed, and we just couldn't get any sort of rhythm together.

"She said you had a bigger dick than Tommy King but not as big as Lucas Williams," she said as she turned her attention to the two slaw dogs on the plate now in front of her.

Later that night when we got back to their house and Dave and Emily got out to take a quick dip in the pool, no one wanted the night to end. Beth and I had another moment in the back seat. This time it was less rushed, and it went a lot better.

"Have you told your sisters about our backseat moments?"

"No, but I think they just assume that me and you have had our moments."

"I am going to miss you, you know," she said as we cuddled afterward. "You are the only intelligent boy I know."

I figured I'd push my luck. "Intelligent and wonderful?"

She paused and then said, "Intelligent, yes. Wonderful? I'm not sure, I'd have to ask Abby Bennett."

The next morning, I got up very early to pick up Dave for his 6:00 a.m. bus east. I borrowed my mom's car with the promise I'd be back in time for her to go to work. She and my dad were going to drive me to school that evening.

I pulled into their driveway and Dave was on the front porch with his mom and dad. His mom was hugging him, and you could see she was crying. He let go of her and did a quick hug with his dad. You could tell he was just as emotional as his mom. He finally pulled away from them, picked up his two duffel bags, and came over to the car and threw them in the back seat.

I waved to his parents as I pulled out of their drive, and they kept waving until they disappeared in my rear-view mirror. We both had little to say as we drove downtown to the Greyhound Station.

At first I couldn't figure out why his parents, as well as mine, were so emotional over us going off to college. We had both had older siblings go to college. But I would later realize that we were the two who went off to college; our older bothers lived at home and commuted. We were going off, living the complete college dream that we had talked about since middle school, and our parents drilled into us.

I parked on Chester in front of the terminal and grabbed one of his bags as Dave grabbed the other. We walked into the building and read the departure times on the wall. We walked outside and found his bus that people were already boarding. We loaded the duffel bags in the luggage department underneath then turned and faced each other.

"Well, my friend, are we ready for some new adventures?" Dave said to me with a big smile.

"I don't know if you are, but I'm definitely ready," I replied. "We had a good run together, didn't we? I don't think I would've changed a thing."

"No, I don't think I would've either." He gave me a brotherly hug, turned around and boarded the bus.

I went and sat in my car and waited until I saw his bus exit the lot and head towards I-90 east. He saw me sitting there and gave me a wave from his seat. I turned on the car and headed home, listening to the radio as REO Speedwagon played "Time for Me to Fly."

From the last scene of the last episode of My Rock and Roll Girl:

My Rock and Roll Girl, Episode 14, Scene 8
You can tell its early in the morning as Connor pulls into Brewster's driveway. You can see Brewster hugging his parents goodbye, his mom is crying and his dad is trying really hard not to. Brewster walks to the car in the driveway and throws both of his bags in the trunk. There is a song playing in the background, an instrumental bridge solo to a song you should know but can't place yet.

Cut to:

On the way to the bus terminal they drive past a lot of the places that were settings in the story so far, including Steve Dogs, Public Hall, the old Agora, and the old Stadium. The car pulls up in front of the Greyhound station, and they both get out of the car. The trunk pops open.

Cut to:

BREWSTER
Picking up one of the bags: "Well, my friend, are we ready for some new adventures?"

CONNOR
Handing Brewster the other bag: "I don't know if you are but I'm definitely ready.
We had a good run together, didn't we? I don't think I would've changed a thing."

BREWSTER
"No, I don't think I would've either."

Cut to:

They give each other a brotherly hug, Brewster turns around and boards the bus. Connor walks back to the car and sits and waits for Brewster's bus to leave.

Cut to:

As the bus pulls out Brewster sees him through his window and gives him a wave.

Cut to:

Connor pulling out in traffic as he turns up the radio, and we hear as REO Speedwagon playing "Time for Me to Fly."

Even before Erin got to high school the legend of the Robinson's sisters record collection was well known. Before Christmas break her freshman year Erin was asked to write about the best albums of 1970 by our school's newspaper. One or both or all three sisters would write that annual column until Beth graduated. They would also take turns writing concert reviews and previews. The following are their top ten columns from 1970, Erin's freshmen year, until 1976, Beth's last Christmas in high school. Erin came up with the rules that there should be at least one album by a local artist, and at least one by a woman performer.

Top Ten Albums 1970 by freshman Erin Robinson

All Things Must Pass by George Harrison
After the Gold Rush by Neil Young

Moondance by Van Morrison

Bridge Over Troubled Water by Simon and Garfunkle

Sweet Baby James by James Taylor

Ladies of the Canyon by Joni Mitchell

McCartney by Paul McCartney

Déjà vu by CSNY

James Gang Rides Again by the James Gang

Abraxas by Santana

Erin picked *Moondance* as her favorite, and *Bridge over Troubled Water* and *Sweet Baby James* as the best albums to fall asleep at night to.

Top Ten Albums 1971 by sophomore Erin Robinson

Honky Dory by David Bowie

Blue by Joni Mitchell

Led Zeppelin IV

Tapestry by Carol King

Pearl by Janis Joplin

The Low Sparks of High Heal Boys by Traffic

American Pie by Dan McLean

Sticky Fingers by the Stones

The Raspberries

Imagine by John Lennon

Erin picked *Tapestry* as her favorite. I say give her credit getting into Bowie and Traffic before most high school kids did.

Top Ten Albums of 1972 by junior Erin and freshman Emily Robinson

The Rise and Fall of Ziggy Stardust and the Spiders from Mars by David Bowie

Can't Buy a Thrill by Steely Dan

Something/Anything by Todd Rundgren

All the Young Dudes by Mott the Hoople

Machine Head by Deep Purple

Young, Gifted, and Black by Aretha Franklin
Fresh Raspberries by the Raspberries
Harvest by Neil Young
Loggins and Messina
No Secrets Carly Simon

It was Erin who was getting us into Steely Dan, and Emily wrote that *Ziggy* will always be her favorite album.

The Best Albums of 1973 by senior Erin and sophomore Emily and freshman Beth Robinson

Friends and Legends by Michael Stanley
Band on the Run by Paul McCartney
Aladdin Sane by David Bowie
Dark Side of the Moon by Pink Floyd
Good Bye Yellow Brick Road by Elton John
Quadrophenia by the Who
The Smoker You Drink the Player you Get by Joe Walsh
These Foolish Things by Bryan Ferry
Suzi Quatro
Billion Dollar Babies Alice Cooper

All three Girls picked *Yellow Brick Road* as their favorite

The Best Albums of 1974 by junior Emily and sophomore Beth Robinson

Perfect Angel by Minnie Riperton
Court and Sparks by Joni Mitchell
The Lamb Lies Down on Broadway by Genesis
Diamond Dogs by David Bowie
Heart Like a Wheel by Linda Ronstadt
Sheer Heart Attack by Queen
Kiss
Dark Side of the Moon by Pink Floyd (really was the album of the decade)

Waterloo by Abba

Desolation Boulevard by Sweet

Emily was really getting into the female vocalists, Beth discovered Genesis, Kiss, and Sweet.

The Best Albums of 1975 by senior Emily and junior Beth Robinson

A Night at the Opera by Queen

Born to Run by Bruce Springsteen

Still Crazy after all these Years by Paul Simon

Fleetwood Mac

Hissing of Summer Lawn by Joni Mitchell

Toys in the Attic by Aerosmith

Face the Music by Electric Light Orchestra

One of These Nights by the Eagles

Family Reunion by the O'Jays

Face the Music by ELO

Both girls picked *Born to Run* as their favorite.

The Best Albums of 1976 by senior Beth Robinson

French Kiss by Bob Welch

Songs in the Key of Life by Stevie Wonder

Agents of Fortune by Blue Oyster Cult

Silk Degrees by Boz Scaggs

Night Moves by Bob Seger

*Dreamboat Anni*e by Heart

Frampton Comes Alive

Boston

Breezin' by George Benson.

The Sanford Townsend Band

Rockpile

Beth, on her own, picks *Night Moves* as her favorite, and give her credit for picking both a Stevie Wonder and George Benson albums. It took us white kids awhile to catch on to that stuff. She also picked eleven instead of ten I think to piss off her older sisters.

By the next Christmas all three girls were out of high school, but they mailed out a Top Ten list to their friends.

Rumors by Fleetwood Mac
Exodus by Bob Marley
My Aim is True Elvis Costello
The Stranger by Billy Joel
A Farewell to Kings by Rush
Changes in Attitudes, Changes in Latitudes by Jimmy Buffett
Stage Pass by the Michael Stanley Band.
I Don't Want to go Home by Southside Johnny and the Asbury Jukes
Eddie Money
Hotel California by the Eagles

Erin picked *Rumors* as her favorite, both Emily and Beth picked *Stage Pass.*

Chapter 2

The years Dave and I, along with Beth, went away to college were priceless. If I told you how priceless, you wouldn't believe me.

We went away to college during the best time ever to do that. There has never been a time comparable to ours, never will. I have taught Freshmen Composition, Creative Writing, and Screenwriting to college students on and off for years. And, before it is all said and done, and I'm done with all that is the movie and TV world, I'm going to walk away and find some college to teach at full time. Someday…

Anyway, we really did go to college at the right time. I used to try to explain this to classes I was teaching, and they all thought I was BSing them. Plus, none of them could envision the world, let alone college, without cell phones and the internet.

We went to college during that wonderful time after the mess in Vietnam had ended, and before the conservatism and educational policies of the Reagan years kicked in. Our parents, as well as our professors and school administrators, were happy we didn't have to deal with the draft and protests. Everyone was happy we were sitting in class instead of dodging bullets in a rice paddy thousands of miles away. And affording college was not the racket that it is today.

The drinking age for beer in Ohio was 18, in states like New York and Florida it was 18 for everything. Since the war in Southeast Asia had finally ended, the sexual revolution started back up full blast. The girls I went to college with, and the ones that Dave went with, were miles different than the mostly Catholic Parma girls we knew back home. It was a golden time for not only college girls but also movies and especially music, and both of our schools believed in the liberal part of the liberal arts. So many things happened at our colleges, as well as colleges across the country, that wouldn't or couldn't happen today. Too many rules, too much has changed. Going away to college went from a life experience to the overpriced mess that it is today that's supposed to produce a 70k job.

The war had just ended it and all the social chances that started in the 60s were now back and center stage. For the first time marijuana laws were being relaxed. Most college students had easy access to birth control, and most parents were happy either way. They didn't know what their kids were up to when away at school and most didn't care.

The creative arts exploded. In music we had periods of roots rock (the Grateful Dead), country rock (the Marshall Tucker Band), jazz rock (Steely Dan), blues rock (Led Zeppelin to Johnny Winter) to go along with the folk and Beatles influenced music of the late 60s and early 70s. Movies that either won or were nominated for best picture from our high school and college years included *The Sting, American Graffiti, The Exorcist, The Godfather parts I and II, Chinatown, Lenny, One Flew over the Cuckoo's Nest, Barry Lyndon, Jaws, Dog Day Afternoon, Rocky, All the Presidents Men, Network, Taxi Driver, Annie Hall, the first Star Wars, The Deer Hunter, Coming Home, Midnight Express, Apocalypse Now, Norma Rae, Ordinary People, and Raging Bull.*

What do the major studios put out today? Batman sequels, Superman sequels, remakes of movies like *A Star is Born* (the fourth one!). How many more major movies do we need featuring the Marvel super heroes? How many romantic comedies do they make featuring characters who aren't too romantic or too funny? Remakes and sequels, that's all Hollywood knows. *Bridget Jones, Bridget Jones' Diary, Bridget Jones' Baby*, Bridget Jones Shits the Bed.

My school fed my love of movies by showing a classic film on the big screen on Wednesday nights. I got to see *Casablanca, A Day at the Races, Rio Bravo*, all the Fred Astaire and Ginger Rogers movies, and dozens of other great movies on a big screen instead of on television. It made a big difference. Plus, believe it or not, once a quarter they included a classic X rated movie, and me and my movie friends saw *Deep Throat, Beyond the Green Door*, and every other classic porn film on the big screen. That's the kind of stuff that doesn't happen today.

Meanwhile, musical albums released from that time period included *Good Bye Yellow Brick Road, Houses of the Holy, Brothers and Sisters, 461 Ocean Blvd., Bad Company, Court and Spark, Diamond Dogs, Kiss, Pretzel Logic, Rush, Rock n Roll Animal, Grievous Angels, What were Once Vices are Now Habits, Living and Dying in ¾ Times, Todd, Get Your Wings, Buddha and the Chocolate Factory, On the Border, The Hoople, Bridge of Sighs, Endless Summer, Elvis Live in Memphis, Close up the Honky Tonks, Welcome Back My Friends to the Show that Never Ends, Starting Over, I Can Stand a Little Rain, Sneaking Sally through the Alley, The Heart of Saturday Night, Sheer Heart Attack, The Lamb Lies Down on Broadway, Fire on the Mountain, Heart Like a Wheel, Blood on the Tracks, Rock 'n Roll, Physical Graffiti, That's the Way of the World, Blow by Blow, Katy Lied, Journey, Will o' the Wisp, Toys in the Attic, Red Headed Stranger, Cut the Cake, Dream Weaver, Fleetwood Mac, Outlaws, Daryl Hall and John Oates, Wish You were Here, Face the Music, Still Crazy After All these Years, Northern Lights, Schoolboys in Disguise, A Night at the Opera, The Hissing of Summer Lawns, We Sold our Souls for Rock and Roll,* and hundreds more.

Name one current song, let alone an album, that people will be listening to 50 years from now?

And don't even get me started on books. Whenever I teach a new class of college kids, I always ask has anyone read any good books lately? If it is a freshmen English class no one raises his or hers hand ever. If it is a class with upperclassmen several might raise their hands. I will then ask how many students have read a book on their own in the last year and nine times out of ten no one raises his or her hand.

When I was in college, college students still read. And if you liked reading, you got exposed to the literary works of the day and the past that made a difference.

It's well documented how most young people don't read today and that's a shame. I fell into a group of book lovers in my freshmen dorm. We remained an unofficial club through our college years, constantly trading books back and forth. A lot of these books I brought home during breaks and shared with Dave and Beth. Some were current at the time; others were forgotten classics from the past. But the books I and thousands of other college kids read for the first time back in the 70s and 80s included *On the Road, The Princess Bride, Zen and the Art of Motorcycle Maintenance, The Drifters, I've been down so long it seemed like up, Even Cowgirls Get the Blues, Gravity's Rainbow, The World According to Garp, Fear and Loathing in Las Vegas, Roots,* all the Kurt Vonnegut books, a whole lot of Hemingway, *The Godfather, Winds of War, North Dallas Forty*, Dan Jenkins's sports novels, *The Drifters*, all the early Stephen King stuff and his Richard Bachman teen books, *Jaws, Jonathon Livingston Seagull, Love Story, Ragtime,* Arthur Hailey's books, *Rich Man Poor Man, The Betsy, The Choirboys, The Day of the Jackal, The Deep, The Exorcist*, Saul Bellow's books, the list went on and on. Someone please find me a college student who reads at least one book a semester!

Recently my niece and her boyfriend did a cross country trip before her senior year in college. They checked all the travel websites on the internet and made a plan to see all the sights. Each night they stayed in a nice hotel, ate in all the best restaurants. They didn't sleep one night in their car, didn't pull the sleeping bags out and slept under the stars in a rest area off a freeway somewhere. They had a game plan and stuck to it.

And that was the problem. Nothing was spontaneous, nothing out of the ordinary was explored. They followed all the travel advice they found on the internet.

Forty years ago, we didn't have the internet to guide us, our travel adventures, as well as our life adventures, were guided by the albums we listened to, the movies we watched, the books we read. They didn't give us set instructions to guide us in our adventures but gave us a sense of adventure that caused us to search out our own adventures, not the same old stuff everyone else did. Those places to go / things to do my niece and her friend read about on the internet were someone else's adventures and experiences done over and over by thousands of travelers.

The end of the war; the accessibility to funding a college education; a great time for music, movies, and the arts; and an overall feeling that college was a life experience as well as an education, not an overpriced process to get the highest paying job or getting into the most prestigious grad school.

College kids now grow up in a cut and paste world on the internet. Instead of going someplace and having some sort of experience, all they want is to take a selfie to post on some website. And when college is over, they want a 80k job with six weeks off and an hour a day to play on the internet.

OK, I'm done ranting, now back to the story…

After high school Beth took a different path in life than her sisters. Just like she told me she would on the night we met, when she was in ninth grade and I was in tenth. Her sisters never left home; she couldn't wait to go away.

We had the most unique relationship, still do, and along with Dave I always considered her a best friend. I can't even count how many times we were lovers, although technically we never dated. We've cried on each other's shoulders through deaths and broken romances, and often were the first ones to share good news with each other. And, probably most importantly, starting somewhere in our college years we knew each other's biggest secrets.

Now you have to remember when Dave, Beth, and I went off to college, there was no internet, no cell phones, no email. Most of my years I shared two phone lines with 40 other guys in a frat house. Beth lived in a house full of girls with only one line. It was always busy. Dave's situation was similar to mine. Through all of this Emily back home became the conduit when we needed or wanted to get ahold of each other.

Emily religiously wrote Dave every week through four years of college. She would semi-regularly write me too. Her letters were filled with news about family and friends back home, and was filled with music news and what bands we were going to see on the upcoming Christmas or summer break. They would include newspaper and magazine clippings about our favorites.

We, being guys, wrote a lot less. But Emily made sure she kept us up to date on birthdays and who to send get well or condolences cards.

Beth and I were at schools that were on quarters, which meant we were away until June. Springtime in central and southern Ohio was awesome. One weekend she asked me to come down, that she had something to tell me.

I never considered any of us the outdoor types, but we ended up camping with her friends at a state park in the hills down that way. On Saturday we went off by ourselves and found an isolated pond with a creek running into it, and we spent the afternoon skinny dipping in the cold water under the sunny skies.

We had sex several ties on the rocks that surrounded the pond. That surprised me a little because she had told me she had had several lovers at school. Oh well, that was just the way it was back then!

We were laying on the rocks getting dried by the sun when she rolled over and curled up next to me and said, "I have something to tell you." That always meant it was nothing she could share with her sisters, even as close as they were. For a moment I thought she was going to tell me she had a three way with two football players.

"I had sex with a girl," she said with a slight smirk on her face. She waited for my response. I definitely was taken by surprise and didn't know what to say, so I said something stupid. "Were her tits as nice as yours?"

She playfully punched me in my upper arm and said, "I share with you my deepest secret and all you could come up with is a tit joke?"

There was a long moment of silence. I rolled over and gave her a hug. "O.K., tell me about it."

"First, I have to say, I'm not turning gay. Bi maybe, but I like having sex with guys too much to give it up."

She told me the girls name was Laurie and, believe it or not, she was a cheerleader with a boyfriend on the football team.

"She likes sex just as much as I do. She said it was her first time too. It just happened walking back to our dorm from a party. Her roommate was gone for the weekend and one thing lead to another."

"Are you going to see her again?"

"We talked about it. It's something her boyfriend cannot find out about. Or anyone else in her world. I guess she doesn't have a best friend like you."

I took that as a compliment.

Beth went on to say Laurie was a real cool kid, but her boyfriend is an asshole. "It's that old high school football and cheerleading thing. They haven't grown past it."

"We'll see what happens when we come back in the fall." She paused. "I know you won't go blabbing this to anyone."

"Well, I don't have a big secret to share with you. I guess I'm leading a boring life."

"Oh, yes, you do. You just haven't come to peace with it yet."

"And what's that?"

"I'm not going to tell you yet, even though it's quite obvious to me and most of our friends."

I had no idea what she was talking about, and I dove back in the pond for one more swim.

The next year Beth and a bunch of her friends met me and a bunch of my friends at a concert in Columbus. It was Ian Hunter, with Mick Ronson, at Vets Memorial, with MSB opening up. This was during

Hunter's "Cleveland Rocks" days, and by the look of the t-shirts in the crowd the whole audience was college kids from Northern Ohio going to school in central and southern Ohio.

It was a great show, and before everyone went their separate ways, we stopped in one of the joints on High Street to have a beer. Beth and I introduced everyone to each other, and when she introduced Laurie to everyone I immediately knew who she was. And, yes, she was sexy in a cheerleading sort of way. Knowing what had happened between Beth and her suddenly gave me a massive hard on. After introductions were over Beth slid up next to me and very discreetly grabbed my crouch. She whispered in my ear, "I knew meeting her would make you horny."

That summer when we were home for break Beth didn't mention her big secret to me once. I kept waiting for her to tell me mine, but the summer slid away and she never did. Oh well, I said to myself, maybe she will tell me at Christmas.

Meanwhile, Emily and her sisters continued to just love music. They weren't very talented themselves, although all sang in the choir at school at one time or another. What they were talented at was buying albums and making cassettes of their favorite songs. They each had their own bedroom at their house, but it was the rec room in the basement that they took over with stacks of records and a Pioneer stereo system their parents got them for Christmas a few years earlier. A couple of big speakers and a couple of old couches and the place was as comfortable as can be.

They just didn't buy albums; they bought great albums. And they didn't just go to concerts, they went to all the good ones. Because of Big Ed's connections they got great seats, as long as they told his secretary what they needed before the tickets went on sale to the general public. The secretary's name was Nancy, and she just loved all three girls. She was also such an important part of Big Ed's job that she was considered a member of the family.

And the girls had this thing that they did. It's kinda hard to explain unless you saw them do it. They would sing or dance along to the music they loved, and they did it together in same rhythm that they looked or sounded as one. Individually they weren't great singers, but together they sounded like real Motown background singers. Over the years I have danced with each of them at a variety of functions and I would say each of them danced O.K. But when they were at a concert and one of their favorite songs was being played they would dance in the aisle together and they would look like a ballet, moving with each other as a whole. It was always pretty cool.

And I saw their finest moment, although they have always brushed it off as just another concert. And I was there, and Dave wasn't. Springsteen played New Years Eve and New Years Day in Cleveland at the old Richfield Coliseum in 1978/1979. Two of the greatest concerts I had ever gone to. Anyway, we all went to the first show but Dave had his grandmother's birthday party the next day and couldn't go.

They had three sections on the floor for both concerts with pretty wide aisles between them. We sat in the middle section on the aisle in the eighth row for both shows. Both nights the girls spent much of the concert dancing in the aisle. This was right after the *Darkness* album came out, and every music lover give or take five years either way of us knew every song on that album and *Born to Run* that came out before that.

Almost the whole concert was a sing along with much dancing in the aisles, everyone was on his or her feet the whole show. Four hours of high energy.

Both nights they ended the show with a cover of the great Gary U.S. Bond's song "Quarter to Three." A great '50s rock and roll song which allowed almost everyone in the band to do a solo, and everyone in the audience to get up and dance. The first night the girls did their ballet act with each other in the aisle, and I think it caught the eye of both Springsteen and Steve Van Zandt the lead guitarist. Somewhere in the middle of the song they both caught the girls act, then looked at each other and laughed.

The next night we had the same seats and the show went pretty much the same, with a lot of audience participation. The girls took over the aisle once again, and this time I knew that Springsteen and Little Steven had both noticed them.

Again, they closed the show with the same great version of "Quarter to Three." Then it happened. During an extended Clarence Cleamons sax solo Springsteen jumped off the stage and joined the girls in their dancing. You would've thought they had been rehearsing all day, Springsteen blended in with the girls and they entertained everyone for a minute or so as they were shown on the big screens at both ends of the arena. Springsteen quickly gave each girl a hug and hopped back up on stage and finished the show. It was a moment none of us ever forgot.

Like I said, I thought that was the girls' finest concert moment, but they always disagreed. They favored the night Southside Johnny dragged them up on the stage at Public Hall, and they sang backup and danced on "Havin' a Party."

Dave was totally clueless when he came home from school as far as his relationship with Emily. While he was away having one big adventure after another, Emily was an office girl counting the days until he was back and helping cousins and friends and workmates get ready for their weddings.

Most of Emily's female friends were Parma girls. A Parma didn't necessarily have to live in Parma, but in the area. She had fun in high school and got a good job afterward working in an office, or bank, or similar situation. She had no desire to go to college, and the next big event in her life is finding a boyfriend to marry. A house and children soon came next. If all of that didn't happen by the time she was twenty-five, she was considered an old maid.

You have to remember at that time Emily was the quintessential Parma girl. Getting married was the next big thing in a Parma girl's life after high school graduation. Starting a family was soon after that. By the time Dave came back from college they had been involved for seven years, a very long time for everyone.

During the years we were college students, she had been in at least a dozen weddings, most of them Catholic affairs with big wedding parties. During the summer when we were home, Dave would be her date; but the rest of the time she would go dateless and that was getting old.

When Erin graduated high school, she became a smaller member of our group. She was too cool to constantly hang around with a bunch of high school kids, but she didn't abandon us either. She often still took us to concerts and always played Mother Hen to her two younger sisters.

Like a lot of girls (by this time young women) Erin made the mistake of falling in love with a musician. But it didn't seem like a mistake at the time.

Luke Farley played in bands in and around Cleveland since middle school. A couple of years older than us, when we got to know him, he was a junior at Cleveland State. He had seen Erin out and about for a couple of years, and even asked her out years earlier at a CYO dance one of his bands was playing at.

"No, I can't," she told him, but the look on her face said that she was interested.

"Why not?" he responded.

"My parents say that I can't date anyone out of high school until I'm out of high school."

"Do you always do what your parents say?"

"Always," she responded with a smile.

"At least give me your number; I'll call you the moment you graduate."

He didn't call the moment she graduated, but soon after.

At first everyone liked him, except for me and Beth. My long-repressed crush on Erin was slowly coming to the surface, and it was getting tested now that she had a serious boyfriend, while Beth kept saying, "There's something about him I just don't like." She could never pinpoint it, but she never changed her opinion.

"I've been watching you play since I first saw you at a dance in middle school years ago," Erin told him on their first date.

He responded, "I've been watching you watch me for just as long."

They became a good-looking couple around town. He played in several bands. His cover/dance band was a local success, having gigs all over town, mostly clubs and college bars. He was also in an original music band that rarely played out but put a lot of time in rehearsing and working on their own material.

His only obvious negative to me (besides being Erin's boyfriend) was that he was a smoker, which had always been a definite no-no to our group of friends. We knew a lot of kids that smoked, but none of us did. The girls had been trying to get their mom to quit for years, and it just didn't appeal to me and Dave. Our parents had all quit years earlier.

He charmed Big Ed and Big Barb. He turned on the personality whenever he was around them. Big Ed was hosting a group of labor leaders for a conference at one of the west side country clubs. That evening they had dinner and dancing with their wives, and Luke put together a bunch of his musician pals to play 50s and 60s oldies, and they were a big hit. He and Big Barb became partners in crime, sneaking Winstons behind the girls' backs. She had tried to quit the whole time I knew her, but she just could never completely do it.

Beth always thought the turning point with Luke came with what was probably his high point as a musician. A mid-level touring band, one that had one top forty hit a few years earlier but spent most times opening for larger acts, needed a substitute guitar player immediately. They played Cleveland two nights, first opening up for someone at Public Hall then getting a club date at the Agora. Luke's cover band opened for them. The next night they played Columbus and their lead guitarist tripped and fell coming off stage and tried to catch himself but instead broke his arm. The band remembered the guitarist from the night before, some phone calls were made, and Luke was hired as a three-month fill in. It almost perfectly fit his school calendar, but it also meant he would be away for most of the summer.

Three months on the road with a real band, opening up for a band who currently had an album on all the charts, was a dream come true for a local musician like Luke. Even though it was only for three months to him it was the real deal.

The offer came when Luke was becoming an adult and started to take his relationship with Erin seriously. He cut his music nights down to 1-2 a week; he made a plan to finish his marketing degree at CSU, and he started to think about getting a real day job. He had a long talk with Big Ed about finding something. "I won't be gone for a long time," he told Erin. "When I come back home, this will all be behind me. Plus, you can come and see us on the weekends."

Erin didn't go and see him every weekend, but she did several times. The first time was to Milwaukee, and she saw them play in a packed arena of 8,000. It was a rush for him, and a big rush for Erin too. When she came home Sunday night, she couldn't stop talking about it. The show, partying afterwards with both bands, meeting all the other girlfriends. She couldn't believe she was with people whose albums she actually saw in record stores.

She couldn't catch up with them until a month later. Things had changed slightly. The show she saw in Tulsa was still great, and Luke played his heart out. But things afterward appeared different. First of all, most of the girlfriends backstage were different. It didn't take Erin long to realize the stories she had heard about groupies weren't completely wrong.

Second, Luke looked haggard. Not real muscular to begin with, he looked lighter than he did in Milwaukee. Most of the people at the post-concert party back at the band's hotel seemed a bit dirty. When Erin came home the next day, she wasn't quite exuberant. But she figured another six weeks or so and this will all be over, and Luke would be back in Cleveland.

On both trips she took tons of pictures; and when she showed them to her sisters, they could not believe how gaunt Luke looked in some of them. When Beth saw the pictures she feared the worst. And she ended up being right.

Somewhere on that rock and roll road from Milwaukee to Tulsa, probably in some seedy fifty-dollar hotel room, an over-the-hill groupie turned Luke on to heroin. She told him about all the great rockers who had done heroin at one time or another. Fentanyl laced heroin had just become the drug of choice of hard partiers, especially those in the music world. Cheaper and more assessable than cocaine, Luke with all of his addiction tendencies was no match for the drug.

By the time he came off the road, Luke looked awful. He spent the first few days at his parents, trying to get healthy and sober. He returned Erin's calls, "I'm just exhausted from the tour; I'll see you soon."

For a few months he tried going straight but couldn't. Erin thought it might be his drinking; she had no idea that it was something worse. Finally, her sisters made her face reality. There was a big confrontation between Erin and Luke, and for the first time, but surely not the last, he promised to get help.

This would be the pattern for several years. Luke would straighten out; Erin and he would be a happy couple, and then for no apparent reason he'd fall off the wagon. One minute they would be talking about a wedding, the next he would be going back into rehab or therapy.

There was no doubt that Erin really loved him, and he loved Erin, but sooner or later there is a breaking point.

I had heard most of this long distance from occasional long distant phone calls with Beth. I spent time around them when I was home on breaks during some of his sober stretches, and I hated to admit that I was beginning to like him. And what was worse, all of this, both good and bad, came while Beth made me realize what my dark secret was.

His addiction problems came and went for several years. The longest he stayed sober was six months, but he just couldn't stick with it. He had a full life, working a good day job, finishing his degree at CSU, playing or rehearsing most nights. He really didn't have much free time; Erin made sure of that. She knew the busier he was, the less chance of falling off the wagon. Every time he did fall off the wagon, Big Ed was able to get him into a top shelf rehab program.

The summer after Dave and I graduated college was one big soap opera. Where do I start? First, both Dave and I graduated and had some money in the bank so we decided not to take a summer job. I spent the summer trying to get up the courage to go out to LA and chase my dreams. Dave was unsure whether he wanted a full-time job, wanted to go to grad school, or maybe attend law school.

By the time we both got home summer was in full swing, and we dived headfirst into it. Baseball games at the old stadium, Thursday nights at the Agora, Tuesday nights at the Madhatter, Fridays at the Parties in the Park, concerts at Blossom. It was like we were still kids, not worried about how adulthood, the real world, was knocking on our doors.

Unexpected stuff was happening all around us. The girls' mom found out what some of the activities were when Big Ed would go on his "business" trips to Vegas. She was not pleased. One of my sisters ran off with her boyfriend, and we didn't see them all summer. Erin's boyfriend went into rehab for the millionth time, and she was getting sick of it.

Then, just as summer was ending and some real decisions had to be made, My Rock and Roll Girl, the car not Emily, was stolen right out of the Robinson's driveway. We were all crushed. In a way the car getting stolen signified our childhood ending and adulthood arriving, whether we wanted it or not. Everyone, including Big Ed and Barb, mourned like we had lost a close friend.

When an old college friend a couple of years ahead of me who did decide to chase the Hollywood dream called and said there was a sofa with my name on it in his apartment, I decided to go. I bought a '67 Chevy Impala with not too much rust or miles on it, threw some clothes in the backseat, and took off. It took me three days to get there, sleeping in rest stops along the way.

My mom and dad supported me, even handed me an envelope with $500 in it as I literally went out the front door. I promised I would call every Sunday night just like I did at school. The girls threw a going away night for me, complete with a finish at Steve's for slaw dogs. When they dropped me off at my house, Emily gave me a hug; Erin hugged me and for the first time actually kissed me on the lips and showed a bit of sadness that I was leaving, more than I expected, and Beth had a few tears rolling down her cheeks. "I'm not crying because I'm losing my boyfriend; I'm crying because I'm losing my best friend," she said. The girls handed me a bunch of homemade tapes for the trip.

Dave got a big surprise when he got a phone call from one of the law schools in New York City to see if they should still hold a spot for him. "I don't know what you are talking about," he told the lady on the phone.

"Well, according to our records all McKenzie Scholars, if they decide to do so, are eligible to extend their scholarships to include law school in New York City."

Dave had no idea. He told the lady on the phone he would get back to her before the end of the day, called the McKenzie Foundation and found the thing about law school was true. To say he was surprised is taking it lightly, and he didn't really know what to do.

He also found out the McKenzie Foundation would not only pay tuition but also give him a stipend to find lodging in the city.

To be slightly fair to Dave, he really didn't know his scholarship, if he met certain goals, also included grad or law school. He kicked ass away at school, being the overachieving asshole he was, and he exceeded all expectations. And the fact that the foundation included not only tuition, but a living stipend almost made it an offer too good to pass up.

Dave did not tell Emily right away. At first he thought he would talk her into coming with him. But then realized it wouldn't work.

"I can't see her being away from her family," he told me. "And being away from her sisters? Beth is the only one out of the three of them that could do that, but not Erin or Em."

It was around this time Beth and I were rolling around on the couch in their basement, doing nothing more than necking like a couple of middle school kids. "You haven't figured it out yet, have you?"

"Figured out what?"

"Your big secret."

"What?"

Her face took a very serious demeanor. "I am so lucky to have you as my best friend. I cherish the fact that we lost our virginities together. But we are going to stop having our occasional friends with benefits moments. As long as we keep falling in the sack with each other every few months will keep you from pursuing your big secret."

"What are you talking about?"

"You are never going to take a serious run at Erin."

Awkward moment of silence. "Is it that obvious?"

"It's been obvious for years."

"But that was just a schoolboy crush on an older woman. Plus, with the rock star in her life, it's never going to happen."

She looked at me again seriously. "I'm not completely sold on that…"

Erin in her own way like her little sister Beth was now marching to her own beat. Already in her mid-twenties, a time when many of the girls she grew up with and attended school with, were getting married and starting families. She wasn't in a hurry for any of that. She wasn't going to settle for the first guy that asked her, or a musician with a drug problem. She kept living at home and worked as an office girl in the accounting department of a manufacturing company. She found she had a way with numbers, and she was promoted to book keeper. She liked it, but didn't love it. But the job fit her life at the time, and she banked most of her paycheck each week. We admired her for how she stuck by Lukas side during his many episodes, but Beth and Emily both told us they thought it was just a matter of time until she put him on permanent waivers. Erin started prepping for that moment.

It was Christmas break my senior year in college. Dave and Emily were still going strong, and everyone, especially Emily, assumed he was going to come home for good when the school year ended in the spring.

I was the only one planning to do something that did not involve coming home for good. I started sending resumes to all the production companies in Los Angeles. I applied to USC and UCLA in case I wanted to attend grad school, maybe part time. And I contacted the few real contacts I had out there in LaLa Land. I was determined to make it as a TV or movie writer. I worked on putting together a notebook of treatments and writing samples.

My dad had two older brothers and a bunch of uncles who were Cleveland policemen. They met up for breakfast at the Red Chimney diner on Thursdays, and sometimes I would join them. There would be usually 8-10 people at breakfast, including some of their buddies who were also retired.

I would just sit there quietly enjoying everyone's company, and keeping my mouth shut and just listening to the stories that were being told. Great cop stories about gamblers, sleazy politicians, murders, murderers, "broads," lost bags of money, and anything else you can imagine. But when I got home afterward, I would try to remember what was said and write down all the juicy details in my journal. A lot of these stories would become the basis for the treatments that I would put in my writing samples.

I also had in my writing journal some pieces based on some incidents of our youth. I had something about when Dave and Emily first met, going to Steve's after concerts, things like that. Never expected anything to come of them, but I need things to show people.

When we went away to college, Dave and I and the next year Beth, at times it seemed like nothing changed. Summer and Christmas breaks were filled with good times. Dave and I still got our summer jobs from Big Ed, and we were making more money than the average college student during breaks. And he always found us a couple of weeks of work over Christmas. God bless the union!

Emmy wrote Dave weekly. She started working as an office girl for one of the companies whose workers belong to the union. Her dad got her the job without an interview. When she walked into the office on her first day of work, the owner of the company immediately saw how beautiful she was, and he immediately posted her outside of his office next to his secretary. Amongst her duties was to greet anyone entering the offices and wanting to see her boss.

By Christmas she was keeping the boss's business and personal calendar and became the company's first ever office manager. She streamlined purchases for the office, and soon was supervising the other six women in the office. There was no animosity towards her, as she had a knack of making everyone else's job easier. She was natural for what she did, and she was a pro dealing with people. That she inherited from her dad. And she was surprised at how much she liked it.

When we were home for breaks, her life revolved around Dave and the rest of our gang. They had our social lives planned out, and we did not object. We seemed to be together most weeks from Thursday until Sunday, starting with college ID night at the old Agora, and usually ending either during the summer in the right field bleachers in old Cleveland stadium following the Indians, or in some bar in December watching the Browns play. There were always concerts and pool parties, but somehow Emily always arranged one night a week when it was just her and Dave. Nothing fancy, drives up to the islands, picnics in the Metroparks, stuff like that.

Emily was the most beautiful girl I knew, inside and out. The only one I knew that compared was her older sister Erin, and Beth wasn't far behind. And, for some unknown reason, and not in a boyfriend/girlfriend way, all loved me.

Erin, Emily, as well as Dave had interesting observations on Beth and her sometimes relationship with me. All three of them just couldn't figure her out when she did her own thing. Being Beth's best friend, I would always defend her, stating that she was just independent and, at times, marched to her own beat.

One time in the spring of my sophomore year, Erin and Emily decided to drive down to Athens to check on their younger sister. They included a short stop at my school to see me. When they pulled up in front of my frat house on a Friday afternoon in the blue Caddy, it seemed like every guy on frat hill decided to come out and see what was going on. They parked the car right in front of our house and both got out of the car and gave me hugs and kisses. They were tanned and blonde and busty with great smiles, and in the hour or so they hung out before getting back on the road, every one of my fraternity brothers was in love with them.

"I thought you were bullshitting us," more than one said to me. Beth had visited a couple of times, and no one believed when I said she had two sisters in the same league as her. Both Emily and Erin had that effect on people, both guys and girls, young people and adults. People fell in love with them; they were just so affable and attractive, neither had an enemy in the whole world.

Meanwhile, Emily just got it at work. When her boss realized how many people came through the office just to say hi to her, or to flirt with her, he gave her a clothing allowance each month. Dozens of mostly men came through the lobby on any given day, salesmen, engineers, designers, most stopping at her desk whether they needed to or not. Some of them would ask her out, but she would just point to the picture of her and Dave on her desk. She was spending more time away from work alone, but she knew it was only a matter of time until we were back home on a break.

She did have a situation she was having a hard time with. Most of her girlfriends from high school, as well as those she met on her job, were Parma Girls. Emily was one of the few in her crowd not directly on that path. She was patient waiting for Dave to finish school.

Erin and Emily could still be seen at every concert or music club, and they would often be hit upon. Both did a good job of deflecting them away, but it started to get old. And then there was the social obligations that need a date, things like engagement parties and weddings. At least during the Christmas season and summers Dave was home, and she loved to go to those types of events with him. But after a while she would break down and ask someone to an event just as friends.

I ended up my college days unattached at school, but had had several healthy relationships with a couple of pretty cool girls. They knew where I was headed after graduation, and that kept either of the relationships from getting too serious. Also, the other reason none of my college romances got too serious was because of my big secret, something that Beth finally made me realize.

After we were both out of college, and when I came home the first time from LA, I proposed once again that we should give it a shot at being boyfriend and girlfriend, even if it was long distance.

"Why not?" I asked her.

"We are not meant to be like that. You are my best friend, not my significant other."

"What do you mean?"

"Think of all the years we have known each other and not just once…" and her voice started to break and her eyes were filled with tears.

"What do you mean not once?"

She paused and then replied, "Not once have you ever looked at me like you look at Erin."

I was stunned, I didn't know what to say.

"Ever since the first time we ever met you guys you have held her on such a, I don't know a pedestal; I have realized I will never be seen by you like that."

I was still stunned into silence. I didn't know what to say.

She kept at it. "And don't tell me she is too old or to pretty or too whatever. I know you better than you do. And I know you are twice the man than those boys she has dated over the years."

Chapter 3

Up until sometime in the 80s, Cleveland, and Cuyahoga County for that matter, were pretty corrupt places. To get anything done one had to weave through a spider web of politicians, union bosses, and old school organized crime cronies.

What broke up this log jam was the changing of the guard on all three fronts. The old school politicians, labor leaders, mafia chiefs were fading away and those that replaced them did not live up to their "standards." The old timers, whether they were on the right or wrong side of the law, did a good job of keeping low profiles. They lived-in middle-class neighborhoods, got involved in churches, drove American made cars.

They were hands on in their jobs, both good and bad. The labor leaders knew many of their members personally, took care of anyone hurt on the job, attended funerals and sent gifts for weddings and births.

All that started to change. The new wave of politicians, labor leaders, and wise guys, started to get greedy. Plus, they had watched too many gangster movies. Having a good salary, a pretty easy job, a couple of trips out a town a year, and the ability to take care of their friends wasn't enough.

Suddenly labor leaders and politicians who were making 75k with full benefits and retirement wasn't enough. These new guys, instead of living in Parma or Euclid or Lakewood, were buying new houses on the water in Avon Lake, country homes on five acre lots in Geauga County, or $500,000 new homes in Independence or North Royalton.

One politician, on his $85,000 county salary, built two houses on Johnsons Island in Western Lake Erie for who knows how much. What small role did we play in this? When the office crew went on one of their "working vacations" to Las Vegas, usually with a few "clients," and we were still around, Dave and I would spend the week working in the office mostly just answering phones and running errands, like dropping off contracts, medical paperwork, things like that.

We would get paid double time on Sundays when we would pick our guys, as well as a few of our bigger clients, up at the airport. Dave would drive the east side guys home in one car, I would drive the west side guys in another car. We would then meet up somewhere in the middle, probably the Red Chimney, to get something to eat, and we would compare how bad the guys smelled, and how tired and haggard they were. Back then we thought it was funny, that it was part of business for the bosses. But we didn't realize these guys weren't a bunch of college kids on a weekend bender but grown middle-aged men looking very bad and smelling from too much Canadian Club and Black Velvet.

Years later in the Cuyahoga County Court House what happened on those weekends away would become public. But back then no one had a clue.

And the occasional trips to Las Vegas became more than a chance to do business. Power and control became too much of the job, doing their jobs took second place. And sooner or later, they made it too easy for the FBI and Federal Marshalls to figure out what they were up too and bring things to a stop.

His McKenzie scholarship allowed for four years of post-graduate work so Dave, being the asshole overachiever he was, not only got a law degree but also a master's in finance. When he was finishing his fourth year, he had no clue on what he wanted to do. Part of him wanted to stay in New York, part of him wanted to come back to Cleveland, and there was also the matter of Emily. His time away they had drifted apart; she started to see other people, but when they did cross paths on his trips home, she let him know that she still wanted them to end up together. And so did he.

While still in law school, he started seeing semi-regularly a woman he had met in one of the upper west side bars. Nothing serious, but she was funny, available, and it was nice to do something with her every few weeks or so, even though she was a fucking Yankee fan. Her name was Veronika. Dave would later tell me that their relationship became very similar to Beth and mines. The best friends, and sometimes lovers. She was finishing her MBA at NYU and planned on moving to Washington and getting a job as a translator. She had lived under her parents' roof in New York through undergrad and grad school and moving to Washington was going to be a big deal to her. She needed to spread her wings. And the fact she was planning her move to DC kept her relationship with Dave at a slight distance, never getting too serious.

He went to several recruiting fairs and even applied a few places. His law school background caused him to apply to places like the Secret Service and the U.S. Marshall's office. The thought of pursuing bad guys appealed to him. But he also applied to several Wall Street firms, citing his MBA in Finance. A few things interested him, but nothing jumped out to him.

He was sitting by himself in the school's law library finishing his last finance paper when a man approached and sat down across from him. He seemed to be in his mid-thirties, dressed in a conservative suit.

"Excuse me, " he said. "I hate to disturb you, but are you Dave?"

"Yes. Can I help you?"

"I'll only take a minute. Do you remember filling out an info sheet for the US Marshall Service this past winter at a job fair?"

"Sorta."

"Well, you did, and we are interested in getting to know you better. Can you spare us some time for an interview before your semester is over?"

Dave figured what the heck and replied, "Sure."

"My name is Frank Stanton, and here is my business card. The address is our office in midtown. How does Thursday at 1:00 sound? I think you are free then."

"How did you know I was free on Thursday afternoons?"

Frank Stanton just smiled. "We know a lot about you, Dave. I'll see you this Thursday. Thanks for your time. And by the way, check the math on that third column on your flow chart in your paper, I think there is a mistake."

Dave looked down at his paper in front of him and sure enough there was a math mistake on the third column. When he looked back up to thank him, Frank Stanton was gone.

Dave entered the office building listed on the business card and found it to be just like the many other business buildings he had been to over his time in the city. He went up to the twentieth floor, and the elevator opened to what could've been an office for any financial or legal entity.

They lead him into a conference room with several people already there, one of them the man who came and saw him earlier in the week. After introductions, Frank Stanton got right to the point. "Dave, you have stumbled into a situation that could be very helpful to the U.S. Marshall's office. Are you familiar with what we do?"

Dave responded honestly, saying all he probably knew was from popular movies and spy novels.

Stanton changed the subject. "You're dating Veronika Brello, aren't you?"

"We've gone out a few times, nothing serious. She is a good friend."

"Well, we need you to make it something serious. Let me explain..."

And Frank Stanton went on to explain to Dave that Veronika did not come from a classic Easter European immigrant background, and her dad was not a successful legitimate businessman but an international arms dealer. Using his American import/export companies as covers, he sold illegal arms to governments, rebels, and criminals around the world.

"I can't believe that," Dave said. "He seems like the nicest guy in the world." And to most people he did. The Brello family hosted Sunday dinners for families and friends, and Dave had attended the last several. Big meals with the kind of things his grandmother use to make, like stuffed cabbage, sausages and kraut, and chicken paprikash. Those Sunday dinners made him homesick for his own Sunday dinners.

Before he left their offices, Frank Stanton, to paraphrase Don Corleone, made Dave an offer he could not refuse.

Emily tried to act nonchalant about Dave staying in New York after law school. He told her it was another once in a lifetime opportunity, and it wouldn't be forever. She was totally unaware of the circumstances, and he would never share them with her. There will be a time in the future where he will tell me he regretted not coming totally clean with her.

She wasn't convinced. "I think we've lost him for good," she said to her sisters. "Who knows what he's going to be doing and where."

In the years where Emily and Erin still lived in Cleveland, Beth finished school and moved first to Virginia as a journalist, and Dave was doing who knows what out east, and I was trying to make it as a TV and movie writer in LA. When I finally made it, and I use that term lightly, I was far from being an overnight success.

It really was a half dozen years of working every shit job I could find and still spend a couple of hours each day working on my latest project. I bartended, landscaped, waited on tables, and worked every minimum wage job in the "industry," from working on catering trucks to sweeping up sets after shoots.

How I kept at it all those years amazes me now. Sleeping on couches, going through 7-8 roommates, my quality of life was terrible. But

I resolved to never give up, that I had stories to tell and someday someone was going to help me tell my stories. I think it was the stubbornness of being a mediocre athlete in high school and college that helped me get through it.

And whenever I did get a chance to pitch my stories and ideas, the one that got the most interest always seemed to be about those "rock and roll kids" in Cleveland. With every rejection it was always suggested to keep at it and develop those stories.

Dave had been playing the role of the happy boyfriend for about a year, spending holidays with the Brello family. I don't think he even went home that whole time, unsure of what he would tell his family and especially Emily about what he was actually doing. But at the same time, he was really enjoying what he was doing. Things were going great on Wall Street; he was on the legal investigation team at a big Wall Street firm. He was what he called a forensic accountant/lawyer, investigating companies before they bought or sold them, or recommended them to one of their clients. It was killing him not to have Emily share in that part of his life, but his 'other job' prohibited it. He wrote her now more than she wrote him, and they talked on the phone. He combined the hours he worked on Wall Street along with the hours he spent on the weekends with Veronica, telling Emily that Wall Street was a seven day a week for at least a year. Plus, he knew of Veronika moving to Washington after graduation would be there soon.

He told me they were coming close to closure on the situation, and he would fill me in on the details when it was all said and done. I didn't know when, but I just knew that his story was something that I would use sooner or later.

In the years after college when I was trying to get a foothold in the writing business out west, I would come home once or twice a year for various reasons. When I did I would often stay with my grandmother, who was living alone in the older part of Parma. I also usually called her every Sunday night to keep tabs on her. My siblings also kept an eye on her; she was a great lady who spoiled all of us when we were growing up. She passed away when I was in my early thirties, and left her estate, what estate, just an old house filled with even older furniture to me knowing that I would divvy its worth up amongst my brother and sisters.

I came home for the funeral and spent several weeks going through the house. I had first planned on selling it; however, I just couldn't let go of it. I kept putting off meeting with a realtor. I did give one of my sisters her car that was parked in the garage that she hadn't driven in years. Surprisingly, it started right up. Also in the garage were the tools left from my grandfather who passed away years earlier when we were still in high school. He worked in the steel mills, but in his spare time he was sort of handy man who could fix, or try to fix, almost anything from cars to wash machines to bicycles. It was a pretty extensive set of tools.

After my sister took the car away, the garage sat pretty much empty except for the tools and an old lawn mower. After a week or two I needed to get back to LA, and the first real writing job with a real paycheck I got working on a cop TV show. On Brookpark Road from the airport all the way to the valley where it turns into Granger Road, there was and still is dozens of scattered used car lots. Some run by dealerships, others by car rental firms, several of them of the 'buy here, pay here' types.

I was passing one of those buy here pay here lots and just out of the corner of my eye I saw it. I recognized it immediately, but still not sure if it really was it. I turned around in a fast-food parking lot and went back to the car lot. It was filled mostly with cars that had seen their better days, and too many Northern Ohio winters. But tucked in the back row, without even a price on it, was a 1970 robin egg blue Cadillac Coupe de Ville. Our robin egg blue 1970 Cadillac Coup de Ville.

I was immediately accosted by a salesman. A used car salesman, but he ended up being a pretty good guy. I immediately asked, "Where did you get it?"

"Picked it up at an auction last year. I was hoping to do some work on it, but haven't had the time."

It was definitely our car. I found the dent on the back quarter panel from where we backed into someone in the parking lot at Blossom after a Heart concert. Then I went to open the driver's side front door, and still visible, but very much faded, written along where the window edge in Emily's handwriting was My Rock and Roll Girl.

"What type of shape is it in?" I asked.

"Not bad. I start it up every month or so and it has no problem turning over. But it needs a lot of work, plus new tires, new brakes, and who knows what else. The engine is good, and the original transmission has been replaced once."

The transmission was replaced when we drove over the median on the off ramp of the inner belt at the East 24th street exit where the old Agora use to be after a David Johansson show.

After a bit of negotiation, we settled on a price. It was only a couple of blocks away, and I made it to my grandmother's with no problems. The salesman was right, the car ran OK, but the tires and brakes and shocks were shot.

I parked it in the garage and had no idea what I was going to do with it. I did know that it became another reason not to sell my grandmother's house.

I never told anyone that I bought it. On my trips back to Cleveland I would occasionally work on it. I also had a few friends who were good with cars and would sometimes get them to fix something. Slowly but surely, over a course of more than a few years, I got it both running well and looking good. I still did not tell any of our old gang that I had it, even Dave, and to be honest with you, I didn't have any real plans for it.

Chapter Four

HBO hit a home run when it first aired *The Sopranos*, the standard for cable mini-series. It would air for seven seasons and won numerous awards. However, many don't know that it wasn't HBO or even cable's first entrée into the mini-series format, and they took some risks and tried out several story lines in the years leading up to the Sopranos. Also, networks like HBO and others were first getting the feeling that the future after cable was going to be streaming. Streaming wouldn't take off for years, but it was on the horizons. And no one probably expected how Netflix and Prime would become big players in the mini-series game, but that wasn't that far in the future.

As I said earlier, when I first got to LA, I really busted my ass trying to break into the film and television world. I worked every and any job that had to do with the industry, from catering to scene clean ups to hauling sets. I made the rounds with my binder full of treatments and sample scripts, attended dozens of writer nights and workshops, and signed up for any free or cheap workshops and classes. Most of my days were filled. On days I didn't have any TV or movie work, I substitute taught.

After a few months I fell into a group of young people around my age who were just as ambitious as me, aspiring writers but also directors, actors, make up people, sound editors, almost any facet of movie making we found someone trying to break in. Those who had been at it for a few years, and had some source of capital, would spend their weekends making independent films in and around the Los Angeles area. I fell in with several of them, and for more than a few years spent almost every weekend or free day working (mostly for free) on someone's independent project. What you got out of it was experience, connections, and favors that hopefully one day would be repaid on your own projects.

After a few years I became pretty proficient at many of the nuts and bolts of filmmaking, whether it was as a camera man, a mike grip, lighting, or how to set up or take down sets. Still working to break in as a writer, I started making a decent living in the movie and TV world.

I met an aspiring director named Steve Mitchell when I worked for free a couple of weekends on a few independent movies he made. No one ever really saw them, but I thought they were pretty good. Steve's work caught the attention of one of the production companies that made mostly cop shows. They hired him to direct several episodes of a then popular network show, and to repay me, he got me a paid job on the set. I took the job with the stipulation that whenever it fit my schedule I could sit in on the writer's room. Steve had read much of the stuff I had been pitching, and he liked my background of coming from a cop family, and he encouraged me.

Six months later I got my first writing credit, and by the next season I was in the writer's room full time, making union wages as a script writer. Even though that first cop series was set in San Francisco, a place I had never been, I knew the characters and their families and how they related to each other.

Steve wanted to do his own series, and be the boss over the whole operation. We would spend nights, many of them in local saloons, throwing around ideas. Back then cop shows were set in either New York or LA, and sometimes exotic places like San Francisco or Los Vegas. We heard through gossip that one of the big production companies was getting set to do a whole series of shows set in Chicago, including not only a cop show but one also about fire fighters. So that ruled out doing a cop show in Chicago.

Cleveland at the time did not have the support services to do a complete show for 14 or 15 episodes. Soon it would, but not yet.

Plus money was a problem. Several of the big production companies liked Steve's work, and several said good things about some of the stories I pitched around town. But to get a show of our own needed a strong financial commitment from someplace.

Steve was asked to direct an episode of the cop show that was going to be set in San Francisco, which we filmed in LA, but also Vancouver, Canada, and was going to film some scenes up there. Steve asked me if I wanted to tag along, and the next thing we were on a plane. We worked pretty much around the clock for a week, and the trip was pretty uneventful except for one thing. We met a woman from the Canadian Government's Department of Film and Television, who was there to oversee the production. She explained what her job was to us, and it piqued both of ours interest.

"You mean to tell me," Steve said to her, "the production company gets a tax break and maybe even a grant by filming up here?"

"Yes. As long as you employ Canadians in all aspects of your production. I mean you can have others, but it has to be 60%."

Steve grew up in Detroit. I grew up in Cleveland. We had both done our time in Canada fishing, going to Niagara Falls, things like that. On the flight back you could tell things were rolling around in our heads, trying to put things together.

A week later my first-generation cell phone rang in my studio apartment in the middle of the night, the first apartment where I didn't have a roommate.

"I got it," Steve said.

"Got what?" I groggily responded.

"Just get to work early today, and I'll tell you about it."

We were about to finish filming the cop show we were working on for the season, and there was some uncertainty whether it was going to get picked up for another year. It was a good show but had pretty much run its time.

Sitting in the writer's room at six in the morning, I knew Steve had a great idea. "Remember what that woman said about working in Canada? Why don't we do that."

"Work on what? Do you have an idea about a show? Are we going to move to Vancouver?"

I could tell he had done some research. And the ideas that we bounced off each other for the next hour would end up changing both of our lives.

It was also around this time that Erin and Beth came out to visit me. Emily didn't make the trip, she was attending a wedding with a guy she had met at work. Since Dave had been drifting farther away from all of us, and very rarely went home anymore, their relationship finally fizzled. It was time to turn the page on certain things, and she had tired of waiting for him to show up full time again.

I was completely unaware at that time what Dave had gotten himself involved with. I thought he was just another lawyer on Wall Street trying to make his millions.

The week with the girls was great. We did a lot of the touristy things, plus they liked to come to work with me and watch the show being filmed. We even got them to be in a big bar scene as extras. We also got them some tickets to see a couple of game shows and to see the *Tonight Show* being filmed.

We did talk about Emily. Beth said it best, "She's not in love with a guy; she's in love with getting married and having kids." Surprising to me, neither one of them was optimistic about Emmy's current relationship. Both Erin and Beth were unattached at that time. Erin had finally got her rock and roller out of her system and was dating a few guys around town, and much to my surprise was now in her second year of nursing school at Cleveland State. She said, "I'm going to have to fend for myself sooner or later." Beth was working as an investigative reporter for one of the first online news networks, not sure which one. I was really proud of both of them, and really enjoyed them being there. And no, I didn't sleep with either one of them! But when I dropped them off at the airport, Beth gave me a sisterly hug and kiss on the cheek, and when I expected the same from Erin, she surprised me with a hug then a long kiss on my lips.

"We miss you guys," she said. "I miss you." Then off she went.

I also remember about that weekend is both of them at different times told me she was concerned about their father. He was really stressed about some things at work, but both of them were unsure of what they were.

A year later we started shooting the first season of *Detroit River Blue*, a cops series set in Windsor, Canada, and Detroit, Michigan. We used an abandoned hockey rink in Windsor as a sound stage and employed mostly Canadian citizens in a variety of positions. The show revolved around mostly Canadians and their families who lived in Windsor but commuted across the river to their jobs as Detroit policemen.

I'll be the first to admit we got lucky, especially finding out about the Canadian government's film and television policies, the casting, the stories we got to tell. It all came together far better than we ever thought. Five years later, when we finished the series, both cities changed so much the series would not have been possible.

After the turn of the century, and especially after 9/11, Windsor took almost a 180 turn. It's a lot different town now. Back in the '90s and before that, Windsor was the wild, wild west of eastern Canada. Downtown on their main strip was a group of strip clubs that were as good as any anywhere, giving its downtown area the name "the Canadian Ballet." Filled with totally nude dancers, some who drove hours to work their shifts. In some of the joints it was cheaper to buy a round of lap dances than to buy a round of top shelf shots. The dancers were as beautiful as the girls who hung out in the clubs in L.A. The drinking age was 18, and there was also every kind of bar imaginable sprinkled between the "gentlemen's clubs," many of them with cheap drink specials and late hours well into the night. All it took to drive over to Windsor at the time from Detroit was to go over a bridge. Semi-trucks and passenger busses had to go through special lanes, but passenger cars just came and went. That allowed many of those living on the Canadian side to commute to work in Detroit factories and auto plants. And it also allowed many cars of young men to travel to Windsor to attend the ballet as part of growing up in Detroit and surrounding areas.

Detroit had yet to make its comeback. The Lions still played up north at the Silverdome, and the Pistons played even farther north in the Palace in Auburn Hills. The Tigers still played in Tiger Stadium; in a neighborhood many were afraid to visit. The casinos weren't constructed yet; Greektown was still a rough and tumble neighborhood, and there were ghettos coming right up to downtown. There were blocks and blocks of abandoned factories and warehouses, great places to set crime stories.

The first thing I did was get more stories out of my uncles and their breakfast buddies. Instead of hanging out at a diner with them, I arranged for a bus to take them to Detroit to see the Indians play the Tigers. We had more than enough cocktails on the bus, and I hired a couple of cute college girls to be servers. I had our writing staff on the bus with recording devices and reporter's notebooks with the instructions to write down or record every story they heard on the bus, whether they made sense or not. The forty or so retired cops on the bus drank every drop of booze we brought; the writing staff got more stories than we could ever use, and everyone had a good time. Tribe won 8-3 in old Tigers Stadium.

In fact, the night went so well that a couple of weeks later, when the Tigers were playing the Indians in Cleveland at Jacob's Field, we did the same thing in reverse. We got forty or so retired Detroit cops on the bus, did everything else the same, and again everyone had a great time. Tigers won 4-3 in extra innings.

Doing the bus trip with the Detroit cops not only gave us a new bunch of cop stories, but also was very helpful for the Detroit lingo we would use in the series, things like neighborhood names, nicknames for politicians, and stories about going over to Windsor to see the ballet.

Detroit River Blue got bought by a cable network that is no longer in business, and got very good ratings and solid reviews. Steve got nominated for an Emmy several times, and won once. I got nominated as a writer also several times, and I also won one. We both made some money from being our own co-producers, and you would've thought I was on top of the world.

But in my personal life I was borderline miserable. The years in L.A. since college flew by, as I was busy trying to get where I wanted to be. But all that obsession with getting ahead caused me to ignore some other parts of my life, especially my love life. I had none, not one even slightly romantic relationship. I dated a lot at first; the city and the TV/movie world is filled with beautiful young girls. But most of them are like everyone else out there, looking for an angle, looking for a contact to get them that next job, that next move up whatever ladder they are climbing.

Plus, like most of us who grew up someplace else, I was really hating living in Southern California. It must have been a great place 40 or 50 years earlier, or even 20 years earlier, but it had become too much of too many things. Too many people, too many freeways, too many cars on the freeways, too many people on the hustle. The only social events I really looked forward to were the events put on by the Southern California Browns Backers where I was surrounded by other dislocated homesick Buckeyes.

At first I dove headfirst into the single scene. With everyone of both sexes looking for their next break there were a lot of casual hook ups. Without really even trying I had flings with girls who became movie stars, and many who came up short. I really missed the friendship I had with the Robinson sisters, as well as Dave who, as far as I knew, was still in New York City. But the dating scene became too much like college, and I slowly drifted away from it.

There is a scene in the great WWII movie *In Harm's Way* when Burgess Merideth's character turns towards John Wayne's character and says, "Don't ever marry a movie actress."

Wayne responds, "You married three of them."

With a grin Merideth responds, "They are like eating peanuts. Once you start you can't stop."

I never married one, but boy did I date them. More than a few broke my heart. I was playing for the most part out of my league. When I finally made my way out west, the circles I ran around in was filled with them.

I just kept on putting all my energies into work and my goals, with an occasional trip back home for a holiday or a wedding. The trips to Windsor to film most of *Detroit River Blue* became longer, just to get out of Southern California.

Steve and I were the hot ones for a while, and between filming our third and fourth season, HBO contacted us. We were hot, but we would still be considered cheap compared to other big name production companies. After talking over several different ideas, they asked me to map out a fourteen-episode season for *My Rock and Roll Girl*. They offered us a contract.

The show was based on my high school experiences, as well as Steve's and a few other friends. There were two best friends, three beautiful sisters dedicated to rock and roll, and a blue Cadillac. Our budget was limited. We shot most of it on a sound stage or in a '50s era LA neighborhood. We hired almost all unknowns, and they made union wage. We had open casting calls and had hundreds of kids show up. We went to Cleveland a couple of times to shoot some exterior shots. We used a lot of our friends but paid them this time. I wrote each episode along with several young kids right out of film school. Steve directed the first episode, but he had some younger people he had been mentoring do the rest of them. From meeting with HBO until filming the last scene of the last episode took only six weeks. *My Rock and Roll Girl* only lasted 14 episodes on HBO. It was one of the many series they took a flyer on when they sensed the upcoming competition from places like Prime and Netflix. Its ratings were never great, and it was years before on demand and streaming services kicked in. However, the reviews, when it did get reviewed, were surprisingly good. For a cast of inexperienced high school kids the quality of talent was surprisingly good. Years later one of the leads won an Oscar, and several would earn Emmy awards.

The thing that made it good, and I still think it was good, was that everything that happened was believable. I wanted the audience to see each character as someone they might have known, and each situation something they might have dealt with. I wanted humor but I didn't want it to be a sitcom. Even though most of the characters were teenagers, I wanted a show that adults enjoyed. I wanted drama, but not a soap opera.

I wanted to show that we were having fun, even though we lived in small houses in middle class neighborhoods; and we didn't live in New York City or Los Angeles or near a beach someplace. Most of the characters didn't have cars, and the ones who did were one mile away from the junk yard. It was going to be about great friends who went to concerts and clubs and ball games and Friday night football games. I wanted the characters to be far from rich, hell some of them weren't really even middle class, and all of their parents for the most part were working their asses off in shitty jobs to make their families happy. I really wanted all of that to come through in the show.

Out of the 14 shows six or seven were straight out of our lives. The first couple introduced the characters and their families, and the backdrop of the story, our school, and the working-class neighborhoods.

I only had one battle with the network management that I lost, and that was the name of the characters. I wanted to keep them simple and real, like Mike and Dave and Tom. Management wanted us to use "new" names, yuppie names with too many syllables, and Dave became Connor, and Mike became Brewster. I argued that when I grew up in the '60s and '70s I knew not one Brewster. Maybe in a yuppie neighborhood in Boston someone might be called Brewster, but in '70s Cleveland, Ohio, no one was named Brewster. They even made me change the girls' names. In tribute to the real Robinson sisters I was going to use Erin, Emmy, and Beth, but they made me change them to Annamarie, Amanda, and Alexandria. I argued there was not one Alexandria in my graduation class, but they still made me change them. They told me that "audience research" showed that names of characters were important, and audiences at the time liked more "sophisticated" names.

The first episode was definitely all us. One of the characters runs into another in the school hallway, sees the Bowie albums that scatter across the floor, and asks him if he wants to go to the Bowie concert that Thursday because she has a couple of extra tickets. The cast comes together and all go to the show which was beyond description and had Steve's Hot Dogs afterwards. The two boys stay up until almost time for school talking about the show, and the girls we went with. Both the show, and its ratings, started to take off.

We even found a great 24-hour diner in a gritty L.A. neighborhood to sub for Steve's. The place was empty from around 4:00 a.m. to 7:00 a.m., and that's when we filmed there.

When I wrote the last episode, I assumed there was going to be another season. When that second season never materialized, many questions were never answered; conflicts were left unresolved.

From the ninth through fourteenth episodes, I took their relationships on a steady climb.

Episode nine the audience got to know the three sisters and their friends, and the boys both fall instantly in love with each of them. Both boys think Amanda was the coolest girl ever, but she was still half in love with her ex-boyfriend who was off to college someplace.

By episode 14 the characters were seniors ready to start college, but in between those episodes a lot happened, mostly happy, some sad, some funny. I recently watched all 14 episodes, for the first time in years, and I'm proud of it. I still think we did a good job and deserved another year.

The last episode ended just like it happened in real life, with Connor finding out about his scholarship becoming available again and the decision he had one night to make. The episode ends with a shot of the envelope from his school being on the kitchen table when we come home that night, and then a montage of him getting on a Greyhound headed east with "Time for Me to Fly" by REO Speedwagon playing in the background.

When it looked like there might be a second season, about 18 months later, I did make a season long outline taking the characters through college and into the real world. But it was too late. A couple of the kids from the show went onto some very popular shows on the networks, another got a big part in a Tom Hanks movie, and several others even went off to college themselves. We would've had to replace just too many characters. So, for a variety of reasons, season #2 never happened so who knows what would've happened after that.

The biggest surprise, at least to me, was its popularity when the complete season was released on DVD. It almost became a cult classic, and not a month has gone by since then where someone searches me out just to talk about the series. They always want to know what would've become next of the characters.

The reaction back home was good, and our old friends the Robinson sisters became mini celebrities. Our old friend Michael Heaton at the *Plain Dealer* did a couple of good articles. But the series wasn't picked up and we went back and finished the last two seasons of *Detroit River Blue*. I was trying to figure out what my next thing would be, but nothing seemed to be jumping into my mind. And then my old friend Dave reentered my life.

Emily was pretty much down in the dumps when Dave did not come home immediately after law school was over. She was getting tired of "opportunities of a lifetime," and that one day he would come home for sure. What hurt her more is how little he talked about what he was doing. There was a time they shared everything together.

It had been almost eight years since we had graduated high school, and for most of the time she had worked in an office where everyone loved and respected her. She finally started to go on an occasional date. There wasn't enough days in a week to fill all the nights she was asked out.

It was just about this time that things started to go south for Big Ed. As the feds broke up organized crime's grip on local politicians and business leaders, local labor unions, honest or dishonest, got caught in the middle, and many things were never again the same.

Big Ed was as honest as they came in his world, but he got caught up in a mess that had been going on since before the Great Depression. The way business and government functioned most times involved too many backdoor deals, too many payoffs and political favors, too many sleazy deals. To keep his union relevant, and more importantly to keep his guys working, Big Ed had to play a game that had gone on for years. However, now too many of the players in the game were greedy, flashy guys who had seen *The Godfather* too many times.

The feds first broke up organized crime's power over the local economy, cleaning up their role in business and construction. The feds then went after local government officials, especially on the county level, and many union leaders like Big Ed got caught in the sweep. His union got charged with price fixing and aiding and abetting, as well as smaller cases of bribery and money laundering. Since Big Ed was the union president, he took much of the blame and got an 18 month sentence.

Before I go any further I must say that the feds cleaned up much of the mess in Northern Ohio, but much of the sleazy dealings and dirty government contract just moved south to the state house in Columbus, where things have never been too clean or honest.

Beth called me to tell me about her dad. "That union was his whole life. When he was doing things like favors for politicians or ghost employees or government contracts, he was just doing things the way they were always done."

"How's Barb handling it?" I asked about her mom.

"She's hanging in there. She has a lot on her plate, but you know, she's a strong woman."

The feds originally tried to get a minimal jail sentence for everyone involved. Big Ed got 18 months, but after four his sentence got suspended. He and his lawyers did not know why that happened, but they were extremely grateful.

The good that came out of it was that Big Ed and Big Barb became different people; their lives no longer dominated by Ed's role as a union leader. Ed took his retirement and started on all the projects he had ignored around the house. Barb started to get more involved in activities at church, and her garden club, and volunteer opportunities around town. The only thing missing from their lives were grandchildren.

Big Barb came home one day and heard someone on the back porch. It was Erin, with eyes full of tears and sadness across her face.

"What's wrong, Baby," Barb asked her oldest daughter.

"I'm sorry, Mom. So sorry…"

"For what?"

"For bringing home all these loser guys I've dated over the years. I should be married by now; I should have given you and Dad some grandchildren by now."

Barb sat down next to her oldest daughter and wrapped her arms around her and gave her a hug. "Listen," she said. "You and your sisters have done nothing but make us proud over the years. You've touched everyone's life who you have met. One of these days the right guy will come along, and you will know it."

For weeks afterward she fell asleep listening to the first Karla Bonoff album and the great ballad "If He's Ever Near." Erin kept asking herself, did he already come near and she blew it?

Dave was one of those people that thought there was one person perfect for each of us, and that was Emily for him and he for Emily. He pushed his luck staying out east too long, and the fact he couldn't share a lot of what he was doing with her, or even me, was catching up to him.

After law school he sorta just disappeared from all of us. He told all of us he was involved in some special project and when it was over he'd come back home for good. But he couldn't tell us what the project was, and that just seemed weird.

I had no idea what he was doing. I was busy doing my own stuff. Letters from the girls became fewer and far between, and we all seemed to be going in our own ways. When we did talk on the phone, it seemed like I did too much talking. He wanted to hear about the starlets and playmates I was meeting. I just assumed he was with some big firm on Wall Street making big bucks and doing all sorts of international trading.

Beth remained single, looking for that one special person. "As soon as I meet someone who looks at me the way you have looked at Erin all these years, and the way Dave always looked at Emmie, then I'll get married," she told me several times.

All of a sudden all of us were pushing thirty and beyond.

Nikola Brello quietly put together an operation that made him rich and powerful, both here in the United States and back in Russia. He was involved in many legit businesses, many having to do with the automobile industry, and one big illegal one, guns and other weapons of war. Years before the term ghost gun became known in America, he developed a system of furnishing ghost guns to armies around the world.

On the surface he had car part factories all around the world, and they would ship parts to auto factories, mostly in Eastern Europe and oil countries. But buried in the auto parts shipments would be parts to also make guns. These parts would be made in his auto parts factories.

The key to his operations were the Russian nationals, many educated in the best engineering schools in America, who worked for him both here and in Europe. In America, not only were they designing auto parts, but were also taking apart the best military weapons our arm forces used, and making carbon copies of the components. In Europe they were taking gun parts made all over the world into working weapons. He had the Russians protecting him in Europe, and he hid partly in America by the Russian Orthodox church where he was a big donor.

The other assets that Brello had were the nationals who he brought over from Russia to go to school in America. He recruited them out of the Russian armed services, bright young men and women whose families didn't have the resources to send them to colleges in Europe. After spending a year or two in the Russian army, who would turn down a four-year scholarship to a college in the United States? And who wouldn't be loyal to the guy who foot the tuition bill?

Adding another layer of protection for Brello and his operation was another shrewd move by using the same engineering schools over and over. A couple of big state schools in the Midwest, a couple of private schools in the east. Schools that appreciated several students every year paying the full tuition. The schools did not have to give financial aid, grants, or scholarships to them. And after five or six years of a dozen or so students at each school got him noticed by administrators. And soon he was a trustee at each of the schools.
Between his connections at Russian Orthodox Church, the colleges where he was a trustee, and support of certain semi-sleazy politicians, mostly Republican but an occasional Democrat, Nikola Brello

insulated himself in America.

Dave's job was to keep tabs on not only Nikola Brello, but his whole family.

As the time between when Emily and Dave saw each other became months instead of weeks, it was Beth who took things in her own hands. Sensing something wasn't right, without telling anyone, she went to New York City on her own. She stayed with an old college friend in Brooklyn, and one afternoon she took the subway up to the upper west side to the last address she had for Dave. She walked around the neighborhood, from Columbus to Amsterdam to Broadway back to his brownstone.

About 6:30 she saw Dave for the first time, as he walked down the steps from his apartment to the sidewalk. He took one of the cross streets over to Amsterdam and went north. Beth was surprised at all the activity on the streets as people were coming and going. There seemed to be a restaurant on every other corner, alternating with small groceries and delis. Many of the restaurants had names that represented the cuisine found inside, and Dave went in the door of a place that had an Eastern European name to it. Polish, maybe. Maybe Slovak.

Beth followed him ten minutes later and got a seat at the bar. She looked in the dining room and saw that Dave was sitting at a table of about a dozen. It was obviously a family affair celebrating something, with an older couple at the head of the table surrounded by couples. Several of the women looked like sisters. It was quite obvious that Dave was attached to one of the sisters. Everyone seemed to be having a good time.

The older man at the head of the table was enjoying himself, but even when he laughed and joked with the others, his face still had a hardness to it. He spooked Beth.

Beth had seen enough. She finished her beer and walked out the door. She was going to walk West 82nd to Broadway and take the subway downtown to meet her college friends.

Meanwhile Dave was sitting at the table acting like he was enjoying himself, but out of the corner of his eye, he saw a woman get up and leave from the bar. He didn't see her face, but from her back and how she walked away he knew who it was.

He went outside and saw her walking up West 82nd. "Beth," he yelled.

She turned around, and he ran up to her. "What are you doing here?" he asked.

"What am I doing here? What are you doing here?"

Dave stood silent. He reminded himself that he couldn't say or do anything that would involve anyone from his life in what was going on.

"I saw how you were looking at that girl. That's how you use to look at Emily."

More awkward silence. "What's all that shit about a 24/7 job? Sure didn't look like it today."

Beth turned and started to walk away. Dave stood there speechless, not having a clue about what to do or say.

Nikola Brello became a wealthy and powerful man both legally and illegally. During the Yugoslav and Bosnia conflicts in the '90s, he shrewdly was able to sell arms to both sides. When the conflict ended with the Dayton Accord of 1995, Brello took his arms business elsewhere, with both sides in confusion and all governments lacking cash to continue.

When it became public knowledge after the war ended that he profited from both sides of the conflict, surviving rebels on both sides pledged vengeance. He had several car parts factories and warehouses blown up, and most people thought that was the end of it.

In the second year of his involvement with Veronika, for Christmas the Brellos were invited to stay at the Russian Embassy in Washington for several days of festivities. With a trunk load of gifts for their friends and their families in Washington, the Brellos decided to drive down instead of catching a flight. Its not that long of a trip. December weather had been milder than usual, plus they would have a car to drive them around the Capital for several events. They secured a stretch limo for the trip, so the Brellos and their three children would have plenty of room. Veronika asked Dave if he would like to go with them, but he declined telling her he had plans to go to Cleveland for the holidays. She was going to spend the days looking for a place to live after she finished her MBA.

They made plans for when they both got back. "Lets go see a show or two then spend a quite New Years Eve at my place," Dave suggested to her.

"Not a bad idea. After three days with my family, I'm going to need something," she joked as they said goodbye to each other. It would be the last conversation they would have.

The following afternoon on a stretch of I-95 in New Jersey, as the limo drove on to Washington, it suddenly blew up in a ball of fire, with all of the occupants killed. Dave got the word almost immediately from one of his handlers at the Marshall's office, and he took the rest of the day off from his Wall Street job and walked aimlessly through Central Park until almost midnight. It was then he decided it was time to wrap up affairs and get out of New York. It would take him weeks to get it out of his system.

Immediately, rebels on both sides of the conflict took credit.

The murder of an important Russian businessman and his family was the lead story on all the national news shows that evening, and front-page news everywhere the next day. It was the beginning days of cable news networks and in Beth's office they had CNN on most of the monitors during the day. She saw the story like most people watching that day, but when they put a head shot of Nikola Brello on the screen she froze. Oh my God, she said to herself, that was the guy that gave her the chills in New York. That was the family that Dave was sitting with. She did not know what to make of it. For a moment she panicked, what if he was with them?

It took Beth a day to track down Dave. "It's all over the news. That was the family you were with when I was in New York, right?"

"Yes, it was," he responded quietly.

"We were worried," she said. "We thought you might've been with them."

"Luckily I wasn't."

A pause then she said, "What the hell were you doing with people like that? That's scary stuff."

"I can't tell you. Maybe someday."

"Were you in love with the daughter?"

"No. But she was a good person."

"And did you know about her father?"

"Like I already said, I can't tell you."

Right before the deaths of the Brello family, Dave and Emily talked on the phone. "Dave, I haven't seen you in almost five months. That's not how people have relationships."

"I know, I know. It's just that I'm tied up with these projects at work, and I can't get away."

"You've been saying that for two years. When is it going to change?"

Long pause.

"I know," Emily said, "Someday. Someday."

Another long pause.

"Listen," Emily said. "We aren't a couple of kids anymore. You have things going on in your life that you don't want me a part of. I think I understand that."

They both knew she didn't, but that's what she said.

And they both didn't talk about the elephant in the room. Dave knew Beth reported back to her sisters what she saw in her trip to New York City.

"Listen, Emmy, one of these days these things I'm involved in are going to be over. Then I'll hopefully be back home."

"You've been saying that for how long? Maybe its time for us both to go our own ways. It's been great, but even great things come to an end. And if you ever want to talk about it then come back here in person, and let's talk about it. But I'm tired of phone calls, and I'm tired of letters."

Another pause.

"Goodbye, Dave."

That was the last conversation they had before she got married to John O'Boyle.

John O'Boyle seemed like the ideal wedding candidate. About Emily's age, and had never been married. From a west side Irish family, he worked in sales for a company that worked in cement and aggregates. Good looking, likable.

He pursued Emily very slowly but deliberately. He asked around about her, and heard about her boyfriend who went off to law school and never came back. He knew a guy or two that took out her older sister, but both times it went nowhere.

He was at the crossroads in his life. Early 30s, not married, stuck in a salesman job that didn't offer a lot of upsides. He, like almost all the other salesmen who came through her office, found Emily to be attractive, thoughtful, and sincere. She was the type of girl he had been looking for, and after the first time he met her, he couldn't get her off his mind.

He had a small account with her company that he wanted to expand. That meant often stopping in and seeing her boss. He knew to get through to the boss he had to go through Emily. To get through Emily he started bringing her small gifts each time he would visit, like a coffee from Starbucks. That is probably when he started what we use to call 'a full court press.' He made it a priority to go after her. It started with the occasional coffee, and that soon progressed to flowers. Then he asked her out for a drink after work, and she saw nothing wrong with that. The next thing you knew she needed a date for a wedding or two and she thought why not him?

As a couple at a wedding, they looked handsome together. Both good looking, and they looked even better dressed up. Next thing you knew Emily invited him to a concert, and Erin seemed to like him.

The smartest thing he did in those early months of chasing after her was doing nothing more than kissing her good night. Sex did not enter the picture for a while.

Emily started to enjoy having someone regular to go out with, especially someone who was a good-looking gentleman. He seemed to like her friends, and she seemed to like his.

It was a wedding one weekend; a company function the next. Then an occasional drink after work, a bike ride through the Metroparks on a Sunday afternoon.

His visits to her office kept up, and one day he asked her to help him. "Can you give me an hour or two after work tomorrow? I'll treat you to dinner afterward."

"What for?" She asked.

"I need a woman's advice." He left it at that. "I'll pick you up out front at 4:30."

He took her to the older part of Parma Heights, north of the town center and south of Snow Road. An area with mostly attractive, older brick homes with well-kept yards.

He pulled into the drive of one of them, and they both got out.

"I just put in a bid on this one, and I really need a woman's thoughts on what to do with the inside."

And when he took her inside any woman would've had an opinion on what to do. They walked through the back door, through a small but well-kept kitchen with classic cabinets, then entered the dining room which merged into the living room. Holy cow, hard wood floors, a higher ceiling than anticipated, and a beautiful brick fireplace along one wall. At one end was a stairwell that winded upstairs to the bedrooms. It was completely empty, and the walls needed a paint job, but it just wreaked of potential.

They spent the next hour talking about paint colors, drapes, furniture, and dining room décor. Emily did most of the talking; John just listened. He wanted her to know that he appreciated each of her ideas.

"Well, let's hope things go my way with the realtor." It was the first serious step, but surely not the last, to win Emily over.

It was just time for Emily to get married; it was as simple as that. She was still in love with Dave, but he seemed to be off in his own world, experiencing all of these "once in a lifetime opportunities," so who knew where he was going to end up.

Like I said earlier she had no shortage of admirers. Everyday dozens of marriage eligible men came through their office, almost all of whom would have loved to get involved with Emily. Many had asked her out, she said yes to only a handful when she needed a date for a wedding or other social event. But her defense mechanisms were soon receding.

She was also running out of single women to go out with. Beth was in Washington working as a reporter, and Erin seemed to have a new boyfriend every week. Most of her girlfriends had gotten married, many had started families. That is why John O'Boyle came in to her life at the right time.

Emily had given up her no dating policy while Dave was away, and had gone out with a few guys but found none of them interesting. Beth thought that it would only be a matter of time until someone did catch her interest. She had met many of the guys who had started to ask her sister out, and they kept on getting older, more polished, and affluent. In his own ways, John O'Boyle fit the bill.

I was still out in LA working on a few things when Beth called from DC. "You going to be around this weekend? I might come out."

"Yes, and you know you are always welcome out here."

"Good. And I'm bringing someone with me."

She had never brought someone with her. I wondered who the lucky guy was. Little did I know…

Friday found me sitting at one of the joints in my neighborhood, waiting for Beth and her friend. Just as I was getting a touch impatient, an attractive woman about my age sat down next to me. She had that 'it' disposition about herself, and a million dollar smile that turned into a great laugh.

Just as I was deciding what witty and charming thing I was going to say to her she turned towards me and said, "Hi, I'm Patty. Beth's friend."

Suddenly Beth appeared out of nowhere, gave me a big hug and said, "I see you two already met."

And that is how I first met my close friend Beth's love of her life. We spent the rest of the evening bar hopping in my neighborhood. Saturday we got up early and went to the beach. Sunday we did a brunch, drank way too many mimosas, then went back to my place for a nap. Sunday night I drove them to the airport for the red eye back to the east coast.

From that first meeting in the bar Friday night until when I dropped them off at LAX, I just knew they were a couple, probably forever. They seemed to complement each other so well, knew when to listen, knew when to laugh. I kept telling myself they were made for each other.

Over the years Beth had kept me up to date on all of her romantic moments; and, yes, some of those had been with other girls, but I knew that this one was different.

While Patty was showering and getting ready to leave Sunday, Beth told me how they met.

They were both working in the media in Washington, D.C. They met by accident because both of them were fed up with the dating scene in DC, too many politicians, too many lobbyists, too many sleazebags. They noticed each other at a couple of media events over the course of a month or two, but never really got to talk to each other until they found themselves sitting next to each other at a bar in Georgetown. After a few drinks they started picking out the men in the crowd who had done the worst job with his hair, whether it was plugs or weaves or a bad toupee. "Is there anything worse than a man in his forties trying to look like he was twenty-five?" Beth said to her new friend Patty.

"Are you kidding me? The worst part about those men is too many think that I'm dying to go out with them!"

It was then that Beth said to herself that Patty was the first interesting person she had met in months, while at the same time Patty was saying the same thing to herself about Beth. Beth then realized that she was looking at Patty, this woman she just met, the way I would look at Erin, or Dave would look at Emmy. Soon, very naturally, Beth leaned over and gave Patty a kiss.

"You mean like when we kissed the first time we met each other? When you were a freshman in high school?" I asked.

"Not really. You kissed like a sophomore in high school kisses. Besides, you may have been kissing me, but you were thinking of Erin."

I was sold on Patty from the first moment I met her, but I was worried about how she would be accepted back home. I mean two openly bisexual women might play well in New York or DC, but in the older suburbs of Cleveland I wasn't sure.

The weekend after they came out to see me, Beth took Patty home to meet the troops. For their relationship to go any further, they needed the approval of Beth's parents and sisters. I wasn't there, but both Emmy and Erin immediately fell in love with Patty. They did a bunch of family things including a cookout at their parent's house on Saturday.

Beth even took her over to my parent's house to meet them. They were both impressed with Patty, and nothing Beth ever did surprised them. They knew she always marched to her own beat. They had always treated the Robinson sisters as their own, and they would support Beth no matter what she ever did. That's what people who love each other do.

Beth was unsure of what her parents thought until her father pulled her aside before they left on Sunday. They seemed to really enjoy Patty's company, but Erin just wasn't sure. Her dad seemed serious when he said, "Your mother and I talked, and we feel the need to tell you something."

Oh no, Beth said to herself, thinking the worse.

Big Ed continued, "Your mother and I made a decision." He paused, Beth still thinking the worse. "We decided that if you ever mess things up with Patty, she will be the one that stays in the family, and you will be gone."

It took Beth a moment to register what her dad said, then she hugged him and thanked him over and over.

Later Big Barb would tell her, "As long as you are happy, we are happy. She's so much better than some of the boys your sisters have brought home recently."

I never took Beth's little dalliances with girls seriously, until she met Patty. If she wasn't going to fall in love with her, I was going to. Funny, attractive, with a sharp wit, much like Beth. They say opposites attract; well, this was just the opposite. They are so much like each other; it is scary.

Meanwhile in New York, Dave was reeling from Veronika's death and Emily's plans to marry someone else. And then he met someone. He told me all about it on the first phone call we had had in a long time. "I really missed the access we had to concerts when we lived in Cleveland. However, I do have access to tickets to many of the things on Broadway, and I started to go to them. Not the same as seeing Pink Floyd or Bob Seger, but I did start to appreciate them."

"I really started to like plays involving Bob Fosse and his style of dance. The energy the dancers and singers had reminded me a bit of the concerts we saw as kids. They started a show just called *Fosse*, and it was like a greatest hits of the dance scenes from his plays over the years. It was terrific. The first night I went with a group of friends from the office, and we sat about a dozen rows from the stage. Over the course of the show, I was enthralled by one of the dancers who was in several of the scenes. She was a touch older than most of the other actors, but she was sexy as hell. She had some charisma. I even thought that when she was on stage, she was looking right at me, like she was performing for me only."

He paused then started again. "After the show, we went to one of those joints not far from the theater district that catered to the after-play crowd. You wouldn't believe it, but our waitress was almost a spitting image of the girl from the play. Early thirties, great smile, sexy as hell. All of the guys in our party, even those with their wives or girlfriends, couldn't help but flirt with her."

Dave kept on talking. "It was a really enjoyable evening and Katie, our waitress, was a part of it. As I was walking out the door, I happened to come by her standing by the cash register. I said to her, 'You won't believe it, but we went and saw *Fosse* tonight and there was a woman in the play that was your twin. Do you have a twin who is an actress?'

She smiled at me and said, "That wasn't my twin…that was me."

I was stunned. "How is that possible?'

"When I first came to New York looking for any part I could find in any production, I was a fulltime waitress here. It seemed like the whole staff was trying to find jobs as actors, dancers, or musicians. Anyway, over the years, even when I have had steady real employment like now, I've stayed on one or two nights a week working the after-theater crowd. It's good money in a town that's too damn expensive to live. I hustle over here a couple of nights a week and grab a few tables and make some pocket money."

"You're too pretty and talented to hustle an extra job."

"Believe me, most of us do if you want to live here. I refuse to live an hour away in Jersey or Connecticut."

"Wow, you learn something new every day."

She smiled at him again. "Do you want to learn one more thing?"

"What would that be?"

She took her pen, then softly grabbed my hand, and wrote on the back of it. "You can learn my phone number in case you want to ask me out sometime."

And for the second time in his life Dave fell in love with someone. Although on the surface she did not have a lot in common with Emily, they shared some traits. They were both bright, had good senses of humor, and were liked by everyone around them.

Their first date was nothing special, burgers and beers at Clarke's on one of her nights off. It was obvious there was an attraction, and from the start they found each other very easy to talk to.

She filled him in on the unglamorous side of the glamorous life in the theater in NYC. "I've had eight roommates in ten years in six different apartments." And her cash flow was inconsistent. "In between shows I've sometimes borrowed money from my parents, not something you want to do in your thirties."

Dave could listen to her forever. Besides being beautiful, she was one of those women as she approached middle age had become more attractive, and she was obviously very attractive to begin with. Maybe because she had to wear makeup constantly on the stage, off stage she rarely wore it. That made her even more attractive to him.

They both talked about how they each lived in the world of non-traditional jobs. The theater was a night time and weekend thing, and sometimes took you on the road for weeks or months at a time.

Working as a "federal analysis," it would be months before he told her what he really did, that sometimes sent him away for weeks on end, and his job also involved working seven days a week.

There was one moment that made a pause in the conversation.

As they dug into their burgers (Cadillac for him, the Clarke for her) she casually asked, "Do you know anyone in the entertainment business? That is, besides me?"

He paused for a moment and then said, "I have a close friend from childhood whose working as a writer, mostly TV, in LA."

"Really, anything I would know?"

He would go on and mention the crime stories I had been working on, the success of *Detroit River Blue*, as well as a movie or two I was involved in as a rewriter.

"I've been on some of the New York filmed cop shows. I wish they would call me more often. It's great money. And you can keep your theater gig at the same time."

He debated whether to say anything else and then he casually added, "He had another show on HBO at one time. It only lasted one season."

"What was it called?"

"You probably don't remember it, *My Rock and Roll Girl*."

"You're kidding me; I loved that show. Me and some of my girl-friends got hooked on it when it came out on DVD. It seemed so realistic; it didn't try to be too melodramatic or too funny. And we were all jealous of the characters."

"Why was that?"

"They all seemed so genuine…and happy."

Dave changed the subject as finished their dinners. His role in *My Rock and Roll Girl* would also not be shared for months either.

Dave had no idea what the future had planned. He planned on leaving both of his New York positions, his only plan was coming back to LA and hanging with me awhile. The deaths of the Brellos told him he wasn't made for the life of a U.S. Marshall, and all the greed and corruption that was permeating through Wall Street started him to sour on that life.

And then suddenly he and Katie were an item at the crossroads. She had an opportunity to go to England and maybe be a star, at least give it her best shot. She was offered the lead in a revival of *Heaven and Laughs* in one of the best theaters in the West End. She was originally going to have a pretty strong supportive role, but the big-name actress they signed to play the lead backed out because of a broken ankle. Instead of finding another big name, the producers decided that Katie would be their best option.

Katie would have to be in London soon after the holidays.

I came home for Christmas like I usually did, not bringing anyone with me. Dave was there too, and he was able to bring Katie. I don't think much of our crowd had ever met her before, but everyone seemed to like her. She wasn't in a play then, because she was getting ready to go to London and a new production of *Heaven and Laughs*.

Patty went to her parents' house in Boston, so Beth and I were the only unattached ones out of our crowd. When we went out several times in a big group, we noticed the same things. Erin's current boyfriend and Emily's husband were always intimidated by Dave and me. That was just a fact. And when that happened they were absolute dicks to the girls.

On the spur of the moment, we decided to go to a Michael Stanley show at the Odeon; both Erin's boyfriend and Emmy's husband decided not to go. I think it was the best time Erin and Emily had in years. They got to be themselves and looking back on it that might have been the moment for each of them that they started thinking about ending their relationships. Beth told me that night they had both been thinking about it for a while.

You could also tell that night Dave and Katie had some decisions to make. She had to be in London by January 15 for rehearsals, and he was involved in an investigation that was going to keep him floating between Washington and New York well into the spring. It was time for both of them to decide what they were going to do for the rest of his or her life.

A couple of months later Dave got a phone call from Beth.

"You guys need to come home."

"Why? We were just there over Christmas."

"Why? My sister's marriage is all but finished; my mom is depressed, and my dad is about to go to jail."

"What happened to Emily's marriage? And it looked like Erin really liked her new boyfriend. They seemed happy at Christmas."

"What happened to both of them is the guys they chose weren't you guys."

She then gave me the update on Emily's marriage. "As I told you before, Emily was more in love with marriage than any of the guys she dated or were attracted to her. She was going to marry one sooner than later. Too bad it was sooner."

"He seemed like a good guy at Christmas, and things were good."

"Do you want the short or long version?"

"Keep it short."

"O.K. He has had several major setbacks in his life, both in marriage and outside of it. First, he was hoping to squeeze himself in some sort of business position in the union, but Big Ed isn't in power anymore. So that never happened."

She paused and then continued. "Second, marriage hasn't been the easy street he thought it would be. He thought they would already have baby number one, with number two on the way. I don't know what the problem is in this department, but I think from the very beginning he was shooting blanks. This caused him to drink a little more than he should."

"How much should he drink?"

"Not much, my old friend. He's really not good at it. And it has really accelerated with Emily's health problems."

Long pause then Dave said, "What health problems?"

Another long pause and Beth said, "Oh my God, you don't know."

"Don't know what?"

And that was the first time he heard about Emily's battle with blood cancer.

Our lives took another turn when Dave came out to spend some time with me. I couldn't remember the last time we had spent an extended period of time with each other. We had just finished *Detroit River Blue*, and I needed a vacation. The last free time we had from the show we did *My Rock and Roll Girl*. I couldn't remember when I took more than a day or two off, so I rented a beach house for a month and just assumed that something else would come along. Steve was pitching some things around town, and we figured something would hit.

I picked Dave up at the airport, and it seemed like immediately that no time had expired since we last saw each other. He got excited when I told him we are going right to the beach.

"How long do you got the place for?" he asked.

"A month. I never have taken a real vacation the whole time I've been out here, and I could really use it. How about you? How much time do you have?"

He smiled. "Believe it or not, last week I had two full time careers. Today, I have one. Soon I'll have zero. I'll explain everything sooner or later."

The first night there we went out to eat, and with each beer we got closer to the things we both really wanted to talk about. I wanted to know what he had been doing all these years; he really did disappear. I sensed he wanted to tell me, but he wasn't ready to. And, of course, there was a marriage we needed to talk about, Emily's. We needed to talk about what happened to Big Ed.

The first few days we took the beach in, as well as the bars and restaurants nearby. It wasn't until the third day together that we started to talk about the things we needed to talk about.

"It's time I told you about what I was doing most of the time in New York, and why I drifted away from everyone," he said as we sat on the deck and looked out over the beach to the ocean. We each cracked open a beer, and then he started to talk and didn't finish for two hours.

We were then both exhausted. He from talking, me from listening. My mind was blown away from what he told me, and I had a brain full of questions to get everything processed. It took another two hours to answer some of my questions, and by then we were both done for the day.

The next day we started on our morning walk on the beach, continued during lunch, and went all the way to happy hour down the road. I was finally getting a semi-clear picture of what he had been going through.

Later that week I woke up one morning, sat down in front of my laptop, and tried to organize what Dave had been doing since the end of law school. I believed all of it, even the parts that seemed unbelievable. I tried to arrange things in chronological order.

Spring of his last year at law school he started taking interviews in two different career paths, Wall Street and federal departments like the U.S. Marshalls and the FBI.

He starts to casual date Veronika Brello, the daughter of a Russian businessman and diplomat.

He gets approached in the school library by someone from the Marshall's office.

Later that week he has an interview, and he realizes that they have had an eye on him for at least a couple of weeks.

They have had an eye on Dave for several weeks, not considering hiring him, but because he was dating Veronika Brello.

He is told that Veronika's dad, an outstanding member of the Russian American community in New York City, was also an international gun dealer supplying bad guys from the Mideast to Eastern Europe. They wanted to know if he wanted to be an informant keeping an eye on what the Brello family was up to, especially international travel. He was encouraged to pursue a position on Wall Street, something that he did on his own with one of the big boys working in their internal investigation and auditing department. He jumped head first into his new career and was soon moving up their corporate ladder. Every month or so he'd meet someone from the Marshall's office and let them know what movements the Brello family had made, especially who went where.

He ends up going on several family vacations to eastern Europe with the family. On one they went to a banquet honoring Putin being prime minister.

He liked Veronika, but didn't love her. His heart was still in Cleveland with Emily.

Dave's second trip out to see me came after he had walked away from both his job on Wall Street and with the U.S. Marshalls. He was unsure of what came next in his life, but he had gone through a lot. He couldn't believe Emily got married, and he couldn't believe that Veronika got murdered with the rest of her family. Katie was off in England and killing it; she finally became a star.

I showed him what I had done with our first conversations. He read the manuscript and said it read like a real novel. "You haven't heard anything yet," he told me as we sat down to continue his story.

For three days he pretty much just talked. I would occasionally ask a question or steered him straight, but what he told me was stuff movies and best sellers were made of. Just like I did during his first visit, I tried to organize things. There was a lot to cover, including some emotional moments.

His involvement with the Brello family became a bigger part of his life, to the point that Veronika's dad asked him if he wanted to come and work for him.

His handlers at the Marshall's office thought it was a good idea, but it would be his decision.

He didn't want to leave his job on Wall Street, and told Veronika's dad thanks, but no thanks. He left the door open, explaining he was learning too much on Wall Street to walk away. Maybe in the future. Emily had called him and told him she was seeing someone else. Dave felt bad that he kept Emily, as well as his family and close friends, away from his life in New York; but it couldn't be any other way. He didn't think Emily's romance would turn into anything serious. In his heart he thought he would be done in New York and back home in a year or two tops.

Veronika was a great girl, a good lover, and a loyal friend. But he didn't feel the same way he felt about Emily. And the stress of keeping his lives separate was getting to him.

Veronika's family got blown up by a car bomb on the way to an event at the Russian Embassy in Washington. Including the driver, six people were killed including Veronika and her dad. It made front page news around the world as he was exposed for being the arms dealer he was instead of the legitimate businessman people thought he was.

That event really put Dave in a spin. He knew Veronika's dad was a bad person, but he really liked the other members of the family, obviously Veronika but also her mom and sister; and it made him realize this 'other job' he had might be too serious for him.

Luckily for him Katie came into his life, and he had a love affair like you see in romantic comedies set in New York. But then she left for London.

Dave and Katie had planned to do something special before she left, but neither of them wanted a big farewell. She had an opportunity to leave for London a week early and did without telling Dave. He came back to his apartment one day and found this letter taped to his door.

Every stage girl dreams of coming to New York and finding love and romance, and I did that when I found you. It has been a New York City romantic comedy, and it has all been wonderful.

But now we are at the crossroads…I need to go to London and see if I can finally become a star, and you need to go home and figure out what you are going to do the rest of your life. I think the first thing you and Mike need to do is take care of your rock and roll girls, who really need it now.

Love Always, Kate

Attached to the note was a list of their favorite New York City romantic movies. It was written on a bar napkin from P.J. Clarkes and had several scratched out before they finalized the list. I don't think it is in any order and was written in both of their handwritings.

When Harry Met Sally
You've Got Mail
Moonstruck
An Affair to Remember, the one with Cary Grant
Hannah and her Sisters
Splash
Breakfast at Tiffany's
Adam's Rib
9 1/2 Weeks
The Pope of Greenwich Village
Dave and Katie (has yet to be made)

Dave took the note and napkin, along with a picture of Katie from *Playbill*, and had them framed. He still has it hanging in his office.

All the years working on cop and crime shows taught me the skills to turn real life events into fiction. Things like changing names and locales and circumstances and minor events in real stories enable many a writer to make a living. The events in Dave's life were mesmerizing; all I had to do is turn it into fiction. The material made it so easy.

Six months later I had a draft of our first novel finished. I was then going to turn it into a movie script; I never thought the novel would do what it did. Dave went back to New York to square up a few things. He wanted to put New York behind him.

I showed the novel to my movie agent, and without telling me she showed it to someone at her agency who specialized in crime novels. That agent, again without telling me, showed it around to a few publishers and the next thing I knew several of the big boys were bidding on it. When my agent got back to me, I couldn't believe the money they were talking. It wasn't John Grisham money, but it was pretty good.

I called Dave and told him. "Are you kidding me?" he said. "Wow. What do you want to do? That's more money than we both make in a year."

"There are a couple of things you and I have to do." I told him about the arrangement I had with Steve Mitchell on our production company, and especially *Detroit River Blue.* "The other thing we need to do is come up with a pen name. Something that can't be traced back to you or even me. I cleaned a lot of things up, but there is still some sensitive and tracible stuff left in the book." We talked back and forth on a few names.

We called the book *Accidently Undercover* and it spent twenty weeks on the *New York Times* bestsellers list. Our pen name became Kelly Wagner, named after Leroy Kelly, his favorite Browns player growing up, and Leon Wagner, my favorite Indian. It has since spawned three sequels, each selling more than the one before.

From the first pages of the first chapter of the first *Accidently Undercover* book:

I woke up in the middle of the night, with that strange feeling you get when you wake up in an unfamiliar place. There was a clock on the nightstand that said 3:05. I sat up on the edge of the bed, and my movement must have woken her up.

"What's the matter, Honey?" she said.

I leaned over and gave her a kiss on the back of her neck. "Nothing," I said. "I just have to go to the john."

"It's down the hall. You go past 3 or 4 bedrooms and a sitting room."

We were staying in the Russian Embassy in Amsterdam. It was the first time I traveled on a trip with her family. It's something I always avoided, but my handlers thought it would be good if I tagged along. The embassy building was actually a former 18th century castle of some sort, probably more of a mansion. We were staying on the third floor; her parents were also on the third. There had to be eight or nine bedrooms with huge bathrooms on both ends of the hallway. There was a sitting room in the middle of the floor filled with expensive furniture and a wet bar.

I was told to just play tourist, and to take as many pictures as possible. I put on my bathrobe and slid my camera into one of the pockets. I walked down the hallway acting like I didn't know where the bathroom was. Most of the rooms were disserted, several were offices the rest bedrooms. I took a quick picture in each.

Suddenly I smelled cigarette smoke, and came upon Ronnie's dad, alone in the dark in the sitting room, smoking and drinking a glass of vodka. I put my camera away, hoping he didn't see it. I really liked the guy and still couldn't believe the death and destruction he was responsible for.

"Michael, my son, please come and have a drink with me."

I walked over to the wet bar, filled a glass with ice and then vodka. I was shaking, hoping he didn't see me using my camera ...

"Listen, I know you guys are throwing me another great opportunity, and I really do appreciate it; but I think it's time for me to go home." He looked around at the five others, four men and one woman, around the table.

"As we told you before, if you want to be reassigned to our offices in Northern Ohio, we can do that."

Dave sat silent for a moment or two. "Did I ever tell you guys in the time I've been with you, what I really wanted to do in life? I mean, I've really enjoyed being an undercover spy and doing all these top-secret honorable things. But as you probably know, that isn't what I started out to do."

They started going over all the opportunities Dave would have if he stayed with them. This was the third time.

"I know I got hired without the usual vetting period because of Veronika Brello…and believe me there was nothing to hide…but we didn't go through the usual 'where do you see yourself ten…fifteen…twenty years down the road.'" Dave paused, making sure he had everyone's attention. "And I think because of everything I went through here that I would definitely be a lifer. But the situation is that there are other things I want to do in my life."

Still silence from the others. "I never told you about my father. How he was a teacher, and he loved it. And then they started bussing, and everything changed. He became a bitter old man, and thank God, finally retired. But for most of my youth he was a happy man."

"Does that mean you want to be a teacher?" the woman he had just met asked.

"I don't know if I want to be a teacher; there was a time I did.

But I do know that I want to be happy like he was before things changed. My family didn't have a lot of money, but we were happy. And I developed a great group of friends. I want to be that happy again. I want to be happy like him and my mom were."

Dave paused and looked quickly at everyone in the room. "I've gotten to live in New York City and Washington D.C., two great cities. But I've never really felt at home in either of them. Great places, but not home."

Frank Stanton, the man who recruited Dave and brought him along talked next. "Dave, you are definitely your own man. That's one of the things that we saw in you in the beginning. We appreciate all you have done for us; and if you ever want to get back into it, we would definitely welcome you."

Everyone got up and gave a hug. The woman who had just met him that day, while she hugged him gave him a kiss on his cheek. "You're a good man," she said to him. "I wish I had the courage of doing what you are doing when I was your age."

"Frank," Dave said. "Can you stay for a moment?"

When everyone else left, they had a short conversation. "I need a favor from you," Dave said to his soon to be former boss.

"Anything within reason. We do owe you for a few things that will remain not talked about."

"There is someone who got caught up in the politics back home when they busted up the mob and the corrupt politicians…" And Dave went on to tell the story of Big Ed Robinson. When he was almost finished, he handed him a folder with Big Ed written on the tab. "He's in the fourth week of an eighteen-month sentence. His health isn't good. He took the fall for a few others. He's a good man, and he needs to get out of prison to get the medical care he needs."

Two weeks later Big Ed was home.

Chapter 5

It had been quite some time that we all found ourselves in town at the same time. Dave and I were enjoying the freedom a best seller gave us, and Beth was home in support of Emmy who was going through chemo treatment for her cancer.

Emmy had an appointment the next day for her last treatment for hopefully awhile. Beth called me and said it would be a good surprise for Emmy if we all drove her to the hospital in the morning, she hadn't seen Dave or me in a while. I realized it might be a good time to show off the surprise I had for everyone in my garage.

I told Beth it would be good if we all met at my house, my former grandmother's house; and we would all show up at Emmy's house in the same car. It seemed like a good idea to her.

The next morning, I had Dave, Beth, Patty, and Erin in my driveway. I kept hesitating until everyone was there.

"I have a big announcement," I said.

They all looked at me quizzically, how could I make a big announcement on the morning of Emmy's chemo appointment?

"We really should be going," Erin said.

"Hold your horses, there is just one thing I have to show you."

I started walking towards my garage, and they followed. No one said anything as I punched in the code for the garage door. I turned around because I wanted to see the expressions on each of their faces.

They all realized what was behind the garage door at the same time. Dave was just stunned. I don't know whose eyes filled up with tears quicker, Beth or Erin.

"Oh my God," Erin exclaimed as she ran and opened the driver's door and got behind the wheel like she still was a kid going to a show. Beth hopped in the passenger's side and immediately noticed the upgrade in the stereo system. Dave looked at me and said, "How did you keep this from me?"

"You never asked what was in the garage, and I figured sooner or later you would wander out there and see it."

Dave and I got in the backseat and I went on to tell everyone how I got the car. How I found it on Brookpark at a used lot; how I bought it cheap, but probably spent six or seven grand getting it back in shape; how I found the box of old cassettes buried in the trunk under the spare, and how a friend out in LA turned them into CDs.

Erin said, "Hold on," and she pulled the car out into the driveway so we could get out and see what the body looked like. The guys I had work on it did a great job, even matching it with the original paint color.

The girls couldn't stop crying, Beth started to say something and just broke down. Erin saw that My Rock and Roll Girl was still on the driver's door along the window edge. She saw that, turned towards me and hugged me and kissed me like she had never ever done before. Patty, who had heard dozens of stories about going to concerts in the car was amazed that such a car really did exist.

We pulled into Emmy's driveway, and Erin hit the horn to let her know we were there. Emmy came out of the front door, locked it, then turned and suddenly stopped in her tracks. The old Chicago song "Make Me Smile" was playing on the car's stereo.

And if that wasn't enough, when her sisters got out of the front seats, and we got out of the back seats, she just lost it. Just as it seemed she was going to faint; her sisters grabbed her and held her up. She just totally lost it.

I wanted to show off the stereo system I put in, so I reached in and crank it up. "Smoke from a Distant Fire" by the Sanford Townsend

Band came blasting out of the speakers. Erin, Beth, and Emily all squealed then grabbed each other by their hands and did their concert dance. Emily was quite animated even though she was about to go through a chemo session for her cancer.

The next thing you knew Erin and I were wrapped up with each other, and Dave and Emmy were having a big moment themselves, somehow falling into the back seat of the car. Erin and I looked each other in the eyes, and then she gave me the kiss I had been waiting for since tenth grade.

Patty and Beth just stood there and took it all in. Finally, after watching Emmy and Dave have their big reunion moment in the backseat of the Cadillac, and Erin and I having our moment, Patty turned to Beth and asked, "What about her husband? What about her boyfriend?"

Beth replied, "Fuck 'em. They don't have a chance; the first team is back in town."

The End

This story is dedicated to Michael Stanley and Eric Carmen. Growing up in Northern Ohio would not have been the same without them. R.I.P.

"Thank God for the man who put the white lines on the highway…"

Fire at Steve's Lunch, a Cleveland icon for more than six decades, claims a big piece of real Cleveland

Mar. 18, 2015, by John Petkovic, *The Plain Dealer*

CLEVELAND, Ohio -- A big, greasy, beautiful piece of real-deal Cleveland is gone. Steve's Lunch, an iconic Cleveland diner that was an Edward Hopper painting and a Charles Bukowski novel come to life, was consumed in a fire Tuesday evening.

"A fryer on the stove in the kitchen caught on fire, and there was no way stopping it," said co-owner Ed Salzgerber. "The customers inside got out and everyone was safe. We were lucky."

The fire started at 5:30 p.m., according to Salzgerber.

"The building is from 1860, and the walls have glue framing," he added. "So it spread quickly."

There were two vacant apartments above the diner. Neither the business nor the building was insured. According to Salzgerber, insurers were unwilling to insure the property due to its construction, age and condition of the building.

Salzgerber was standing on Lorain Avenue, looking across the street silently as Cleveland Fire Department crews tended to the smoldering, burned building that housed Steve's, located on the corner of Lorain and West 50th Street.

"It's such an institution," said Salzgerber, pointing at the gutted shell of that beloved institution. "Now, look, you can look right through and see the sky and the building behind it."

For decades, the 24/7 Steve's was a late or last or early

stop for night owls, graveyard-shift workers, cops, cabbies, scruffy rock 'n' rollers and party girls in leggings and tops that were often tighter than tourniquets.

Steve's started rocking around the clock on April 16, 1953, a full year before Bill Haley even released his ode to the 24/7 life. It used the same recipe for its sauce for more than 60 years -- a recipe created by original owner Steve Spanakis.

Steve's, you see, was more than a diner. It was a place out of time, from the old-school counter to the vintage Seeburg Consolettes sitting on the counters. They played vinyl 45s, which spun in the basement of the joint, with the sound running through a wire into the machine. The milieu and homey atmosphere made it a destination -- one that attracted stars including Drew Carey, Bill Cosby and George Clooney.

Some of the lesser-known visitors were even more impressive -- like the man who drove up from Tennessee to buy five dozen hot dogs with everything on it. He said he wanted to take them home and freeze them, so he can have them for a long time.

In almost 62 years, Steve's was only closed twice -- in 1963, the day after John F. Kennedy was assassinated, and for a few days in 1972, after a fire.

* * *

Greg Cielec lives in Cleveland's Brooklyn Centre neighborhood, and is a free-lance writer, novelist, and micro-publisher. He is the author of the novels *My Cleveland Story, A Poem on a Bar Room Wall,* and *My Rock and Roll Girl;* and the novella *Home and Away Games.* Over the years he has been a sports columnist and music and theater reviewer for several publications and websites. He has also been involved in the publishing of dozens of books, as an editor, proofreader, co-writer or publisher. Until recently he was the Academic Advisor for Athletes, an Assistant Football Coach, and an English Professor, first at Thomas More University in Crestview Hills, Kentucky, and then at St. Thomas University in Miami Lakes, Florida. He has taught and coached at a variety of high schools and colleges over the years. He is a graduate of Padua Franciscan High School, Ohio Wesleyan University, and Cleveland State University.

David Hostetler is a resident of Cleveland's Little Italy neighborhood where he is a photographer, graphic artist and publisher. After graduating from Kent State University, he taught high school at James A. Garfield and Streetsboro high schools, where he also coached football and track. David taught journalism at Streetsboro for twenty years, while advising the high school's publications, editing the *North East Ohio Education Association's* newsletter and writing sports columns for Gateway Press. David was one of the first teachers in the America to teach journalism and Desk Top Publishing on first generation Macs. Under David's supervision, both the school newspaper and the year book at Streetsboro were considered amongst the best in Ohio, and won numerous regional and national awards. Dave has designed and edited many projects outside of education over the years, among them Greg Cielec's novels: novels and memoirs written by others; a cookbook, a calendar for the Little Italy Merchants Association; a book of poetry written by homeless men; and a variety of other projects. If you go to dinner at one of the restaurants in Cleveland's

Little Italy there is a good chance Dave designed the menu you pick your meal from.

Kristi Gunyula ia an illustrator and designer based in Ohio, where she lives with her two teenage daughters. Curently completing a duel master's in Counseling and Art Therapy, she draws inspiration for her work from time in her studio, staying active outdoors, and traveling to new places.

Greg Cielec and David Hostetler together have a micro-publishing house called Pink Flamingo Press and Creative Endeavors. Not only do they publish their own works, but quality efforts by others. Together or separately, they have helped with a cookbook; a book of poetry written by homeless men; several first novels; several memoirs; made menus and newsletters for a variety of establishments and businesses; and a variety of other projects. One thing most of their clients have in common is not having an internet store to sell their products. To alleviate this, they have just started an online store at www.pinkflamingopress.myshopify.com. It's still a work in progress, and features not only their publishing projects but also music CDs from some popular regional musicians. If you think you have something to sell that fits the spirit of their online store, or you have an idea for a published work, contact David (RogueDH@aol.com) or Greg (cielec@hotmail.com).